SARAH AND THE SECRET SHEIKH

BY

MICHELLE DOUGLAS

MILLS & BOON

First published in Great Britain 2017
By Mills & Boon, an imprint of HarperCollins*Publishers*
1 London Bridge Street, London, SE1 9GF

Large Print edition 2018

© 2017 Michelle Douglas

ISBN: 978-0-263-07328-7

MIX
Paper from
responsible sources
FSC
www.fsc.org FSC® C007454

This book is produced from independently certified FSC™ paper to ensure responsible forest management. For more information visit www.harpercollins.co.uk/green.

Printed and bound in Great Britain
by CPI Group (UK) Ltd, Croydon, CR0 4YY

To my Auntie Ellen and Uncle Reg
for letting me run wild on their
Mount Vincent property when I was
a wee, small thing…and for trusting that
I'd neither inadvertently drown myself
in the dam or be eaten alive by the wildlife.

CHAPTER ONE

SARAH SLID ONTO a stool and held her hand up for a high five as Majed passed on the other side of the bar. The palm-on-palm contact from the sexy barman sent heat ricocheting up her arm.

His raised eyebrow told her he was intrigued and she had to tamp down a laugh of pure, ridiculous exhilaration. His briefly raised finger told her to give him a moment while he served someone down the other end of the bar.

She settled onto the stool. She'd happily wait a hundred moments to share her news with him.

A hundred moments?

She rolled her shoulders and shook out her arms and legs. Maybe not a *hundred* moments. It wasn't as though she thought of Majed in *that* way. Even if he was sexy as all-get-out, with his dark hair, tawny skin, and eyes as dark as a desert at midnight. She bit back a dreamy sigh. Eyes that were edged with long, dark lashes that should be wasted on a man but weren't in this case as they only made him look more exotic.

But no. It wasn't because Majed was hot with a capital H that she'd quite happily wait until closing time to tell him her news but because she knew he'd *understand*. An easy-going friendship had sprung up between them over the past year when she'd barely been paying attention and she gave thanks for it now.

He prepared the order for the three women at the far end of the bar—mojitos—with a casual elegance Sarah envied. The women all flirted with him—flashing smiles and cleavage with a good-natured abandon that had Sarah biting back a grin. He said something that made them laugh, looking for all intents and purposes completely at ease, yet she sensed he held some part of himself back.

Majed: man of mystery, man of contrasts. He managed this bar but he didn't drink. He attracted women in droves—and some men—and was equally pleasant and courteous to all. He could have his pick from the beautiful people who frequented this inner-city Melbourne bar but she'd never seen him go home with anyone.

Mike, her best friend's older brother and the

owner of the bar, had asked her to keep an eye on Majed, to give him a hand if need be. As he was letting her crash at his swanky inner-city apartment for the six months of his current overseas sabbatical, it had seemed little enough to promise in return. Mike called her his house-sitter but, as he had no cat to feed or houseplants to water, Sarah had secretly dubbed herself his charity case. Mike had simply taken pity on her.

Pity or not, she'd jumped at the chance to cut forty-five minutes each way from her daily commute.

And keeping an eye on Majed had proved no hardship at all.

Mike had mentioned that he and Majed had gone to university together. She knew where Mike had gone to university. Majed should be a banker or a businessman or some hotshot lawyer. Like Mike, he should have a whole chain of bars, restaurants and resorts across the world—or at least be working towards it. What he shouldn't be doing was twiddling his thumbs behind some bar in Melbourne.

Oh, right, and you think you're qualified to be dispensing vocational advice, right?

She winced.

Good point.

She knew all about treading water in a job that was going nowhere. She knew all about not living up to her potential. She ought to. Her mother reminded her of it every single time they spoke.

Majed moved back down the bar towards her and she resolutely shoved her mother's voice out of her head.

'Your usual?'

Her usual was a glass of house white. She straightened and rubbed her hands together. 'I'll have bubbles, please.'

That eyebrow rose higher. 'Celebrating something?'

She laughed because she couldn't help it. 'I can't drink alone tonight. Let me buy you a drink.' He opened his mouth but she cut him off. 'Be a devil and have a lemon squash on me.'

Shaking his head, he did as she bid, and she noticed that at her end of the bar his smile was more relaxed and his shoulders swung a little freer. The fact he relaxed around her loosened the hard knots that the working day had wound up tight inside her.

He slid a glass of bubbles in front of her and she promptly clinked it to his glass of squash. 'To the fact that I am now officially a single woman again.'

Stunned midnight eyes met hers and his smile, when it came, was low and long and sent a spiral of heat circling through her belly.

He leaned towards her. 'You did it? You broke up with Superior Sebastian?'

Ah...not exactly. Sebastian had been the one to dump her. But it came to the same thing— she was single and rid of the awful boyfriend. And Majed looked so happy for her...he looked *proud* of her. It had been an age since anyone had looked at her like that, so she didn't have it in her to correct him.

She pointed to herself. 'Free woman.' That, after all, was the material point. She then waved her hand through the air, assuming supreme indifference. 'I've kicked his sorry ass to the kerb. Never again, I tell you.' And she meant it. She was having no more of Sebastian's on-again, off-again mind games. She couldn't even remember why she'd put up with it all in the first place.

Majed took a long pull on his drink and she couldn't help but notice the lean, tanned column of his throat and the implicit strength in the broad expanse of his shoulders. He set his glass down. 'Never again?'

She shook her head. 'Never.'

'Cross your heart?'

She crossed her heart. In one smooth movement Majed leaned across the bar, cupped her face in big, warm hands and then his lips slammed down on hers in a brief but blistering kiss.

When he eased back all she could do was stare.

He frowned. 'I shouldn't have done that.'

She tried to marshal her scattered wits, tried to corral her racing pulse. 'Oh, yes, you should.' She found herself nodding vigorously. 'You *really* should've done that.'

Whatever he saw in her face chased his shadows away. He shrugged, and she swore it was the sexiest thing she'd ever seen. 'I couldn't kiss you when you were going out with another man.'

Majed had wanted to kiss her? If she'd known that, she might've broken up with Sebastian sooner.

Her heart pounded. 'I was an idiot to put up with Sebastian and his so-called *"this is for your own good"* sermons for so long. It's just...' It was just that sometimes she was *hopeless*.

Majed folded himself down on the bar until he

was eye-level with her. 'You will get his voice out of your head right now and you won't let it back in. You hear me? You do *not* need to lose weight. You do *not* need to wear more make-up. You do *not* need to do your hair differently. And there is absolutely nothing wrong with ordering a fluffy duck rather than a martini, because you *don't* have to be too cool for school, Sarah Collins. You're perfect just the way you are.'

She stared at that mouth uttering those delicious words—words she sorely wanted to believe—and her chest coiled up tight and her mouth dried. She glanced up and moistened her lips. He watched the action and midnight eyes glittered and sparked. Her blood pounded so hard it made her thighs soften. 'Now I want to kiss you,' she whispered.

'That wouldn't be wise.'

But he was staring at her lips with unadorned hunger and he didn't move away.

'Perhaps not, but it'd be fun.'

He gave the tiniest of nods in acknowledgement.

She lifted her chin. Mike *had* asked her to keep an eye on him. 'When was the last time you had fun, Majed?'

His pupils momentarily dilated. 'A long time.'

In those eyes she saw unexplained pain before heavy lids lowered to block it from her sight.

She sat back and surveyed him. He'd been counselling her for months now, telling her she deserved something better than a constantly critical boyfriend. And he'd been right—she did deserve better. And so did he. The way he was going, he'd work himself into an early grave.

She pursed her lips. That might be an exaggeration. She was rubbish at the work side of things but she could make up for it on the play side of the equation. 'Do you ever drink?' she asked.

He straightened. 'I'll be back.'

He moved away to serve a customer. When he returned he folded himself down into the same eye-level position. Did he know how sexy that was? Did he know she'd only have to close the space with a small forward movement to kiss him? If she did…

'You have very speaking eyes.'

His grin was full of temptation. It was all she could do not to swoon—or kiss him. She settled for grinning back at him instead. 'I'm feeling happy, free…and in the mood for some fun.'

She'd never been this bold before, but she

couldn't find it in herself to regret it. She'd made a fool of herself over far less worthy things.

She shrugged but she doubted it was one of those confident, nonchalant gestures all the cool girls managed. Something in the gesture, though, made Majed's face soften. 'What can I say, Majed? I like you.'

He was quiet for a long moment and just when she'd started readying herself for a hot squirm of embarrassment, and the shame of a kindly worded rejection, he said, 'Brandy. Sometimes, late at night when I'm home alone, I'll indulge in a small glass of brandy.'

Her heart grew so big it blocked her throat, leaving her temporarily unable to speak. Finally she swallowed. Air flooded her lungs and her blood danced. 'Maybe you'd like to have a brandy with me tonight? When you're done here?'

He reached out to wind his finger around a lock of her hair. 'There's no maybe about it. I'd like it very much.'

Ooh! Ooh! She found it impossible to form a coherent thought.

He gestured towards the far end of the bar to the waiting customers. 'Don't go anywhere.'

'I'm not going anywhere.' She couldn't believe

how strongly her voice emerged when the rest of her felt as weak and shapeless as smoke. Well... it felt weak until his smile sent her floating up towards the ceiling.

Sarah stretched and encountered a warm male body.

She opened one eye to find Majed sending her a low, sexy smile that warmed her blood. Her other eye flew open as the events of the previous night flooded her. Their love-making had... Wow! She gulped She hadn't known it could be like that.

'Good morning.'

She couldn't contain a grin. 'From where I'm lying, it's a *very* good morning.'

She lifted a hand to trace the firm contours of his bare chest. Majed sucked in a breath. And then three loud knocks pounded on her front door. Her hand stilled. Majed raised an eyebrow.

She lifted a finger to her lips. 'If we're quiet they might go away.'

The knocking started up again.

And again.

Majed's lips twitched. 'They don't seem to want to give up.'

She bit back a sigh before pointing a finger at him. 'Don't go anywhere.'

He brought her finger to his lips and kissed it. 'I'm not going anywhere.'

She slipped on a robe and belted it at her waist. 'I'll be back. *Very* soon.' She'd get rid of whoever it was in double-quick time.

And then maybe they could resume last night's…delights.

Majed shucked up the bed, resting his hands behind his head. The sheet threatened to slip beyond his waist. All she had to do was grab the sheet in one hand, tug, and…

If it were possible, Majed's smile grew wider and sexier. 'Answer the door, Sarah.'

Oh, yes! The sooner she got rid of her unwelcome visitor the sooner she could get back to bed…and Majed.

It was all she could do to contain a shimmy when she flung open the door.

'What the hell took you so long?' Sebastian barrelled into the room.

Her jaw dropped and then she pointed back the way he'd come. 'Leave, Sebastian. Right this moment. We've nothing to say. We're done, so just please go.'

'Hey, baby, don't be so hasty.'

He tried to take her in his arms, but she side-stepped him. Majed had been *so* right about Sebastian. Why hadn't she realised that sooner?

Because you wanted to annoy your mother.

'Aw, Cuddles…'

'Don't call me baby and do *not* call me Cuddles!' God, how she loathed that nickname. It made her sound like an over-fed cat. A neutered over-fed cat. 'We have nothing—'

'I'm sorry, baby. I know I was awful yesterday. I'd had a terrible day at work. I didn't mean what I said, and I don't want to break up with you.'

Had she honestly fallen for this tripe in the past? 'I don't want you to want me back, Sebastian. What I want is for you to leave. *Now.*'

He frowned evidently baffled. Shame, hot and queasy, made her stomach churn. When had she let herself become such a pushover? When had she decided to settle for so little?

He straightened and moved towards her, determination glinting in the hard twist of his mouth. Good God, did he mean to kiss her into submission? If he tried it he'd find himself on the floor clutching his groin. Her mother had taught her about men like him.

'If you touch the lady, I'll be forced to take action.'

Majed leaned against the doorway to the bedroom, wearing nothing but a pair of snug cotton trunks—royal blue—that did nothing to hide his…impressiveness. Her mouth dried at the sheer magnificence of six feet of honed muscle lounging in the doorway, waiting for *her* to come back to bed. A sigh of pure appreciation rose through her.

Sebastian stared from Majed to Sarah and back again. It would've been almost comical if his surprise hadn't been so darned offensive. Finally he swung around and called her a one-word name that made her flinch.

With the casual elegance she envied, Majed strode across and landed a right hook to Sebastian's jaw. Hauling him off the floor, he dragged him to the door and flung him out into the hallway before closing the door on him.

He did it efficiently. Like a trained warrior. And Sarah had no hope of getting her pulse back under control. 'Um…thank you.'

'You're welcome.'

Her heart thundered in her ears. Would it be really poor form to push Majed back into the bedroom and have her wicked way with him? Or should she offer him coffee first? Actually, she had no intention of doing anything without his signal consent because...

She swallowed. Because at the moment he looked seriously forbidding.

She gripped her hands in front of her and prayed for her fantasy lover—the Majed of last night—to come back.

'You lied to me.'

She blinked. 'When?'

'You told me you'd dumped him.'

She swallowed, her hands twisting together. 'I told you I was a free woman.'

'But you deliberately let me believe the break-up was at your instigation, yes?'

Her heart sank. She had. He'd been so proud of her...and she'd wanted to revel in the sensation. She refused to compound the lie with another one. She couldn't speak, so she nodded instead. She wished he'd smile. She tried for levity. 'Are you going to punch me on the nose now?'

He did smile, but it was the kind of smile that made her heart ache. 'I would never do anything to hurt you, Sarah.' He strode over and lifted her wrist to his lips. 'I've had a wonderful night.'

She did what she could to swallow the lump that tried to lodge in her throat. 'So did I,' she whispered. 'But from the look on your face, I'm guessing this is goodbye.'

'Yes.'

He let go of her hand and it felt as if she'd been cast adrift on an endless grey sea. 'Goodbye... for good?'

He nodded.

'Even though I didn't instigate the break-up, I wanted it just as much as Sebastian did. I was relieved that it was over.'

'So why do I now feel as if you were searching for a distraction last night to take your mind off your hurt?'

That wasn't true! But she could see he wouldn't believe her. She'd ruined it—ruined the chance at something amazing—with one careless lie. She tamped down on the sob that rose in her chest. 'I messed up.' *Again.* 'I'm sorry.'

'Ah, Sarah.' For a moment regret stretched through his eyes. 'You're on the rebound, and I'm in an impossible situation. There really wasn't anything to mess up.'

He kissed her cheek and then strode back into the bedroom to dress. Sarah stumbled into the kitchen to make coffee and try to formulate a plan to salvage something from the situation. The click of the front door told her not to bother.

She walked back into the living room and stared at the closed door. With an effort, she straightened and pushed her shoulders back. Majed was right. Great sex didn't automatically make for a great relationship.

For heaven's sake, she didn't need a boyfriend. What she needed was some time alone to get her head straight—work out what she really wanted. It might be for the best if she didn't drop into the bar quite so regularly this week. Maybe not drop in at all for a couple of weeks.

But the thought of not seeing Majed at all caught at her in a way that made her ache. Not to have the chance to chat with him or share a joke…

She dragged both hands back through her hair. 'No, Majed, you're wrong. I did mess up. I messed up bad.'

Majed sensed the exact moment Sarah walked into the bar.

Even though he had his back to the door.

Even though it was a Wednesday night and she

hardly ever came into the bar on a Wednesday night.

Not that she'd shown her face in here all that often in the last six weeks.

He set a Scotch and soda in front of the customer he was serving, took their money and gave change, all the while readying himself for the jolt of seeing her. He glanced towards the door. She'd stopped to chat to a table of her friends—other regulars—and he did what he could to ignore the clutch low down in his gut. She'd had this effect on him from the very first moment he'd met her. In all likelihood she'd have it on him till the day he died. Some things were just like that—desert sunsets, palm fronds moving in a breeze, the scent of spices on the air...and the sight of Sarah.

It didn't excuse the fact he'd been an idiot to go home with her. He should've resisted the temptation. After all, he'd managed to avoid desert sunsets, date palms and spice markets with remarkable ease.

He pushed the memories away—memories of home. They might haunt his sleeping hours, but he refused to dwell on them when he was awake.

He pinched the bridge of his nose. He still couldn't believe he'd relaxed his guard so much.

It was just…

He grabbed a cloth and vigorously wiped down the bar. She'd made him feel like he could be someone different—that he *was* someone different. When she spotlighted him with those pretty blue eyes of hers, she made him feel worthy. And, God forgive him, but he'd been too weak not to revel in it.

The man at the far end of the bar tapped his empty beer glass. Majed got him another. He bent down to check the stock in the fridge. But, rather than rows of wine bottles and mixers, all he could see was fragments from the night he'd spent with Sarah. They replayed through his mind on an endless loop—the curvaceous length of her leg, the way her body had arched to meet his, the taste of her. They drew him so tight, his muscles started to ache. That night had been spectacular—unforgettable.

But the morning after…

He straightened in time to see her laugh at something one of her friends said. Her stupid lie—it hadn't even been a big lie—had reminded him of the mistakes that lay in his past. His hands clenched. Mistakes he had no intention of repeating.

And it had reminded him of all that he owed his family. He forced his hands to unclench. Where on earth did he think a romance with an Australian woman could go? He grabbed a tray of dirty glasses and stacked them in readiness for the dishwasher. If he wanted to redeem himself in the eyes of his family he'd have to submit to a traditional marriage—a marriage made for political purposes that would cement democracy in his beloved Keddah Jaleel and ensure peace for future generations.

Love for his homeland welled inside him. He missed the desert night sky. He missed walking beneath the date palms on the banks of the Bay'al River. He missed the bustle of the undercover markets, the air heavy with the scent of clove and nutmeg. He missed...

His throat started to ache. When he returned— *if* he returned, *if* his father ever countenanced it—Ahmed wouldn't be there to greet him, and he didn't know how he could bear to live there without his brother. He didn't know how he could meet his father's bitter disappointment every single day, or how to assuage his mother's heartbreak. He missed his homeland but he didn't know how he could ever return.

And yet for one night Sarah had made him forget all of that. He hungered now for the respite she represented—the respite she would probably still offer to him freely if he asked for it—but he had no right to such respite. And the thought of making love to a woman who was in love with another man was anathema to him. Pride forbade it.

He lifted his chin and didn't pretend not to see her as she made her way towards the bar…and him. 'Good evening.' The words growled out of him and she stopped a pace short of the bar. He could've bitten his tongue off for sounding so damned forbidding. He tried to inject a note of friendliness as he flipped a coaster onto the bar in front of the nearest stool and said, 'Your usual?'

She eyed him warily as she slid onto the stool. 'Just a lemonade, please.'

It might be a work night but that had never stopped her drinking before. Not that she ever got rollicking drunk. She'd once told him she drank in an effort to anaesthetise herself to the mind-numbing mundanity of her life. It had made all the sore places inside him ache.

Fellow feeling—that was what he and Sarah had shared from the first.

And attraction. At least on his part. It had been instant. And insistent. And it had had nothing to do with his covert—and not so covert—scheme to rid her of Superior Sebastian.

He set her lemonade in front of her. 'Has Sebastian been giving you any trouble?' Was she seeing him again?

She paused in the act of reaching for her drink. 'Good God, no. Not since…'

Not since Majed had thrown him out of her apartment?

'And good riddance to him.' She drank deeply and then shot him a mischievous, if half-hearted, grin. 'Sebastian who?'

He wished he could believe her. She deserved better than the likes of the Sebastians of this world. He took in her pallor, the dark circles under her eyes, and wondered how long it would take her to get over him. 'You're better off without him.' Sebastian had never been worthy of her, had never appreciated her the way she ought to be appreciated.

'I know.'

He could almost believe her…

'Look, Majed, I didn't come here to talk about Sebastian. I—'

She broke off to bite her lip. Something in Majed's gut coiled at the way her gaze slid away, at the way she compulsively jiggled her straw in her drink. 'What have you come here to talk about?'

She glanced around the room. It was a quiet night but there were still a dozen people in the bar. 'It's not the time or place. I was hoping to talk to you once you'd closed. Or…some other time when you're free.'

He didn't want to be alone with her. He folded his arms. His right foot started to tap. 'Can't you just tell me now?'

She stopped jiggling her straw to fix him with a glare. 'No. You deserve more respect than that. And so do I.'

Her gaze slid away. Again. She had a lock of hair that always fell forward onto her face. She'd push it back behind her ear, but it would always work its way free again. Majed held his breath and waited… He didn't release it until it had fallen forward to brush across her cheek. That silly, defiant, joyful lock of hair could always make him smile.

Stop it!

He continued to gaze at her. She didn't look like other women. At least, not to him. Which made no sense at all because, of course, she looked like a woman. And while she wasn't stunningly beautiful, she drew his gaze again and again. He found her...lovely.

Her hair was neither gold nor brown, her skin was neither fair nor olive, and it had taken him a while before he'd realised her eyes were a clear brilliant blue, but once he had he couldn't forget them. Her features were regular, though some might claim her mouth was too wide, but nothing about Sarah immediately stood out. Not physically. Except... She exuded warmth, as if she housed her own internal sun, and everything about her made his fingers ache to reach out and touch her. He had to fight the urge now, and the effort made his muscles burn.

But... There was something in the set of her shoulders.

It hit him then, why she was here, and his hands slammed to his hips. Her eyes caught the movement...followed it... The pink of her tongue snaked out to moisten her full bottom lip and he went hot all over. He cleared his throat. 'You've lost another job.'

His rasped accusation had her gaze spearing back to his but the heat continued to circle in his blood. Her cheeks went pink but, whether at the accuracy of his accusation or the fact he'd caught her staring, he didn't know.

'Well, yes.' One shoulder lifted. 'But that's not what I came to talk about either.'

No?

She stared down her nose at him. 'Mike told you to keep an eye on me, didn't he? He told you to give me a job if I needed one.'

He had, but Majed had no intention of admitting as much.

'Don't worry, Majed, I haven't come to beg you for a job.'

He gave thanks for that mercy. If he had to work with her day in and day out, he didn't know how he'd manage to keep from touching her.

'Mike asked me to look out for you too, you know?'

He jerked upright. 'I don't need looking out for.'

A smile hovered at the corners of her lips. 'Oh, that's right. I forgot. You're an island unto yourself.'

That was *exactly* what he had to become if he was to ever return to Keddah Jaleel, and the fact she found the idea so nonsensical irked him. Sarah was more than happy to tell anyone who'd listen that she was a complete flake, but she had a perspicacity that was remarkable in its accuracy.

'I don't need looking after either, despite appearances to the contrary. I might be a flake...'

There she went, putting herself down.

'But I'm an independent flake.'

'I don't consider you a flake at all.'

She gave a short laugh. 'I'm going to ask you to hold that thought in the forefront of your mind when we have our conversation.'

What on earth had she come here to discuss?

He stiffened. Was she leaving Melbourne? Had he somehow left her feeling that she had to leave?

Damn it all to hell!

He strode into the middle of the room and clapped his hands together. 'Excuse me, everyone, but something has come up and I need to close early. Can I ask you all to finish your drinks and leave?'

When he'd locked the door behind the last customer he spun to face Sarah. 'What did you want to talk to me about?'

She stood and wiped her hands down the sides

of her trousers. 'I think you should come and take a seat and—'

'Stop fudging! Don't delay any longer, Sarah. Out with it.'

'Fine!' She folded her arms and stuck out a hip. She swallowed but lifted her chin. 'I'm pregnant.'

For a moment her words made no sense. He even momentarily revelled in the relief that she wasn't planning to leave Melbourne. 'You're—' he rubbed his nape '—pregnant?'

She nodded. 'That's right.'

'And...?'

She flopped down to her stool. She lifted her arms and then let them drop back into her lap. Her mouth trembled and her eyes were full of fear, sadness, tears and, strangely, some laughter. Her eyes contained the entire world. 'And the baby is yours, Majed.'

CHAPTER TWO

THE SHOCK OF brandy hitting the back of his throat had Majed jolting back to himself. It was only then he realised Sarah had pushed him into a chair, had poured him a snifter of brandy and was urging him to drink it.

He did what she demanded because he was at a loss to know what else to do. *She was having his child!*

'I know it's a shock.' Sarah moved to the chair opposite. 'And I didn't mean to blurt it out quite so baldly.'

But he'd ordered her to.

Heat scored through him, followed by a wave of ice. He stared at her. Was she okay? It didn't matter what kind of shock he might be experiencing, it had to be far worse for her. Physically he was exactly the same as he'd been before she'd told him the news. But, regardless of what decision she made, Sarah would never be the same again. He had to focus on what she needed from him—and do his best to provide it.

She was pregnant with his child!

He opened his mouth but before he could speak she said, 'I understand your reservations concerning the baby's paternity.'

She thought his silence indicated that he didn't believe her?

She'd lied about instigating the break-up with Superior Sebastian.

She wouldn't lie about something as big as this.

'Sarah—'

'Please, just let me explain. It's taken me this long to screw up my courage and now that I've started I'd…I'd rather just keep going.'

He gave a terse nod, hating the thought that she'd been afraid to tell him her news.

'So, the thing is…' She drew a loop of circles in the condensation of her glass. 'Sebastian had mumps when he was fifteen, which means the likelihood of him being able to father children is pretty slim. But, besides that—'

She broke off to stare at her hands. He reached out and wrapped one of his hands around both of hers. She had such small hands, and every protective instinct he had surged to the fore. 'Don't be frightened of me, Sarah. I'm not angry. Just stunned.' He made his voice as gentle as he could. 'I want to help in any way I can.'

Her lips trembled. 'That's lovely of you.'

'You've had a lot to bear on your own. I want you to know you're not alone now.' *She was having his child!* He forced himself to swallow. 'What were you saying about Sebastian?'

'Oh.' Her lips twisted. 'Before we broke up… for the two months before we broke up… Sebastian and I…'

'Yes?'

She disengaged her hand from his to rub her nape. 'We hadn't been intimate.'

He'd always known the man had rocks in his head. This simply confirmed it.

'I don't doubt your word.'

The little moue she made informed him she didn't entirely believe him. 'We'll have a paternity test done to put your mind at rest. If I decide to keep the baby.'

If. His heart clenched at the word, though he wasn't sure why. A child was the last thing he'd expected at this point in his life. It should be the last thing he wanted.

But the ultimate decision rested with Sarah. It

was her body and he'd support her whatever she decided to do.

'Are you and the baby healthy?'

'The doctor says so.'

'You've been to see a doctor? That's good.'

She frowned. 'You're taking this very calmly.'

Inside he was a mass of conflicting emotions but he refused to reveal them. 'We're in this together. I want you to know you're not alone. Between us we'll sort it out.'

Her mouth opened but no words emerged.

'Have you eaten this evening?'

She wrinkled her nose. 'I haven't had much of an appetite.'

He rose and took her hand. 'Come, I'll make you an omelette.'

He switched off the lights to the bar and led her upstairs to the flat above.

'You can cook?' she asked when he'd seated her at the breakfast bar of his open-plan kitchen-dining-living room.

'I make omelettes that are out of this world.'

She glanced around and he wondered what she made of his bachelor pad. 'An omelette sounds kinda nice.'

It wasn't until Majed pulled the eggs from the

fridge that he remembered pregnant women were supposed to avoid certain foods. What about eggs? He swung back. 'Will you excuse me for a moment?'

He sped into the bathroom and pulled his phone from his pocket to open his web browser. He typed in his query and then read down the list of foods that pregnant women shouldn't eat. Right—the eggs shouldn't be runny. Okay, he'd cook the omelette a little longer than usual... Actually, he might cook it a lot longer than usual, just to be on the safe side. Hard cheeses like cheddar were fine too. Right. He snapped his phone shut. He'd keep it simple with a plain cheese omelette. Well cooked.

Sarah tried to find some trace of Majed in his flat—in his furniture and in the décor—but... Well, it was all very comfortable and commendably tidy, but something was missing, though she couldn't put her finger on what it was.

'What do you think of the place?'

She glanced around from the window that overlooked the busy inner-city Melbourne street to find Majed surveying her from the doorway. And just like that her heart started to jackhammer.

'It's nice.' She ignored his raised eyebrow to add, 'I've always been curious to see up here.'

He stared at her for a bit longer. 'The bathroom is just down the hall on the left.' He pointed back behind him. 'And the bedroom is at the end of the hall. Feel free to take a look.'

'Oh, no, I'm all good.' She couldn't invade his privacy that much.

She slid onto her stool again when he started clattering pots and pans and whisking eggs. She knew they were skirting around the main topic of conversation but...dear Lord...the shock on his face when he'd finally realised what she'd been trying to tell him. It made her stomach churn just remembering it. She wanted to give him a chance to get a little more used to the idea before they launched into a discussion about what they would do.

Frankly, she had no idea what that might be.

He moved with easy grace in his compact kitchen and it was no hardship to watch him rather than make small talk...or think. He started to slide her omelette onto a plate, and then jerked, as if he'd burned himself. His gaze speared hers before he seemed to recall himself and finished serving her food.

She stared at the plate he pushed in front of her and had to fight a frown. This did *not* look like an out-of-this-world omelette—it looked flat and rubbery. And brown. Her stomach gave a sick little squeeze but she gamely forked in a mouthful. He *had* gone to all the trouble of making it for her.

His hands went to his hips as he watched her eat. It only made her stomach churn harder. She set her fork down. 'What?'

'Did you lose your job because you're pregnant? They *cannot* fire you for being pregnant.'

She picked up her fork again. 'True. But apparently they can fire me for calling the manager a weasel of a bully who's nothing more than a boil on the backside of the universe that's in dire need of lancing.'

He choked. 'You didn't?'

'I did. And I can't begin to tell you how utterly satisfying it was.' But now she had no job. And she had a baby on the way. Could her timing have been any worse? Talk about irresponsible!

She blew out a breath. She was such a screw-up.

Just ask Sebastian.

Just ask her mother!

'Eat your omelette,' Majed ordered.

She didn't know if it was her self-recrimina-tions, or if the eggs hadn't agreed with her, but she only just made it to the bathroom before los-ing the contents of her stomach. Majed held her hair back from her face while she was sick. He pressed a cool, damp cloth to her forehead, and through it all she wished she felt well enough to feel even a modicum of embarrassment.

Eventually she closed the lid of the toilet and sat on top of it. The concern in Majed's face caught at her. She tried to find a smile. 'Did you know that *morning* sickness is a misnomer? Apparently it can happen at any time of the day.'

'It's...*wrong*!'

'It's certainly unpleasant.' But her legs finally felt steady enough to hold her so she rose and rinsed out her mouth. 'Majed, I know we have a lot to talk about, but I'm feeling beat and—'

The rest of her words stuttered to a halt when he lifted her off her feet and into his arms. 'You need to rest, *habibi*. It's been a difficult day for you. Sharing with me your news has been nerve-racking, yes? We have time yet to talk and make decisions.' As he spoke, he carried her down the short hallway to his bedroom. Very gently, he lowered her to the bed. She had an impression of vast luxury and comfort and had to bite her lip to prevent a sigh of pure bliss escaping as softness enveloped her.

'I shouldn't—'

'Of course you should.' He pulled off her shoes.

'Maybe just a little rest,' she murmured as he pulled the covers over her.

'Rest for as long as you like,' he murmured back.

'Majed?'

'Yes.'

'What did that word mean—*"habibi"*?'

'It's a term of endearment…like "sweetheart".'

A sigh fluttered out of her. She suspected it would be rather lovely to be his sweetheart for real.

Sarah woke as the first fingers of dawn filtered through the curtains of Majed's bedroom windows. She lay still and listened intently but couldn't sense any signs of movement throughout the rest of the flat. Very quietly, she pushed back the bedclothes and tiptoed into the living room to find Majed sprawled across the sofa that barely contained his bulk, fast asleep.

Most people when they slept looked unguarded,

younger...vulnerable. Not Majed. If anything he looked slightly forbidding and stern. It suddenly struck her that the easy-going façade he assumed every day at the bar might be exactly that—a front.

Or maybe your news has given him unpleasant dreams.

She scratched her hands through her hair. How long had he sat up last night, churning over her news? She'd had a few extra days to get used to the idea. Yesterday evening her sleepless nights had finally caught up with her. She felt rested and well now, though, and she didn't have the heart to wake him.

A shiver shook through her. When she got right down to it, how well did she *know* Majed? Barely at all. She had no idea if he wanted a child. She gripped her hands together. For all she knew, he might welcome a child with unbridled enthusiasm. Or the idea of fatherhood might be a total anathema to him. Surely one should know these things about a man before becoming pregnant by him?

Your mother didn't.

Perhaps not, but she didn't intend to take her parents as role models. They'd spent her entire childhood using her as a pawn in their war to score points off each other. That was the only thing she was certain of—that she wouldn't do that to any child of hers. If she had this baby she'd do her best to ensure its childhood was happy and carefree—not a battleground.

If.

Slipping onto a chair at the dining table, she lifted her feet to the seat and hugged her knees. She and Majed had to decide what to do about this baby and she had no idea where to start.

A pen and notepad rested in the middle of the table. She pulled them towards her with the thought of writing a list of pros and cons. She'd start with the cons, because there were so many: the pregnancy was unplanned, she was unemployed, so how would she support not just herself but a baby as well? Her mother would have a fit and there'd be no end to the recriminations. Her father would take the opposite stance and think an unplanned pregnancy was an inspired idea. She was only twenty-six—there was plenty of time yet before she needed to start thinking about having children. She was a total screw-up and surely a child deserved better than that for a parent?

There'd be more cons—lots more—but the length of the list had started to dishearten her. She needed something in the pros column to balance it out…just a little bit.

She stared at the page and bit her lip. There had to be one reason to keep this baby. A solid logical reason that made perfect sense. Her throat ached. The page in front of her blurred. She reached out and wrote a single sentence:

I love this baby already.

She stared at the words she'd just written and blinked hard. She did love this baby, but was it enough? A child deserved a better home than Sarah could give it. But, no matter how much she might wish to, she couldn't draw a line through that single entry on her 'pros' list.

Perhaps she should try a different tack and list all of the options available to her instead. Biting back a sigh, she turned the page…only to find that Majed had made a list of his own. Her heart started to pound. Would it be an invasion of privacy to read his list?

Invasion or not, she had no hope of stopping herself.

At the top of the page in bald, ugly print he'd written a single word: *abortion*.

She couldn't stop herself from flinching, even though it had been the first option that had occurred to her too. Even though it was an option she was still considering.

Beneath that he'd written: *adoption*. She swallowed. Did she have the strength for that? If she loved this baby then wouldn't she want the very best for it? Wouldn't she fight to give it the very best, regardless of the cost to her personally?

She froze when she realised that was *exactly* what she'd do. She loved this baby. All she had to work out now was what would be in the baby's best interests.

She pulled Majed's list back towards her. Two hard, dark lines separated those first two items from the rest of his list. Pulling in a breath, she read on...

Majed watched Sarah's eyes widen as she read down the list he'd made. He knew when she'd reached the end of the list because it wasn't possible for her eyes to go any wider.

She glanced across at him and saw him watching her. Something arced in the air between them before she gave him a brave little smile that cracked open something in his chest and started up an ache that he feared would never go away.

He couldn't afford to fall in love with this woman. He couldn't afford to fall in love with anyone. Love clouded one's judgement. And when one's judgement was clouded it put the people one cared about at risk.

He couldn't fall in love with Sarah, but he could look after her.

'Good morning,' she whispered.

Her voice emerged on a rasp, as if her throat was dry, and he threw off his blanket, rose and strode to the kitchen. 'Let me get you something hot to drink. You should've helped yourself.'

'I didn't want to disturb you.'

He came back with glasses of apple juice and steaming mugs of herbal tea. His body cried out for strong black coffee but, if Sarah was avoiding caffeine the way most pregnant women he knew did, then it would be cruel to drink it in front of her.

He nodded at his list. 'I tried to cover every possible option I could think of. Are there any you've thought of that I've missed?'

She shook her head and sipped her tea. He

watched carefully for any signs of nausea but she merely closed her eyes and inhaled the steam as if welcoming the warmth into her body. Her clothes looked rumpled from having been slept in, and she had bed hair, but beneath all of that a vitality and vibrancy that had been lacking yesterday had started to emerge.

'You've thought of things that hadn't occurred to me.' She pointed to the very last item on the list. 'That's a bit over the top, don't you think?'

He shrugged but his gut tightened. 'My purpose was to list every option I could think of, without making value judgements.'

He'd spent a lot of time in the West. Four years in the UK at Oxford University with trips to the USA in the summer breaks. For the last four years, he'd worked in Australia. But he'd grown up in Keddah Jaleel—a world of ancient tradition, arranged marriages and duty. He knew exactly what his family would expect of him in this situation.

He had no intention of forcing those expectations onto Sarah but...

'I want you to know that whichever one of those options you settle on, whichever you deem is in your and the baby's best interests, I'll support you one-hundred percent.' He didn't want her to doubt that for a moment.

She set her mug down, a deep furrow marring her brow.

'What?'

'Your happiness is just as important as mine.'

He didn't deserve happiness. He didn't say that out loud, though. It was a sentiment that would horrify her. He nodded at the list. 'None of those options make me unhappy.'

Her raised eyebrow told him she didn't believe him. She pointed towards the top of the list. 'This line here is rather dark. It looks angry. Does that mean you hate the idea of abortion and adoption?'

He tried to keep his face unreadable. 'I've no ethical objection to either. It's just...' He reached out and wrapped her hand in his. 'It's just, I don't dare care for the life growing inside you if those are the routes you're considering.'

She stared at him with such intensity his mouth went dry. The pulse at the base of her throat pounded and he could feel an answering throb start up at the centre of him.

'You care about this baby?'

The question was raw, Sarah's voice full of

heartbreak and hope, and he didn't know which one would win out.

He nodded. There wasn't a single doubt in his mind that if Sarah had this child—*if*—he would love it with everything that was inside him.

Then tell her that. You need to give her more.

But he didn't want to pressure her one way or the other.

She winced. 'Majed?'

He realised he was all but crushing her hand. He loosened his grip immediately and massaged her hand gently before releasing it. 'Last night I found myself getting excited about the prospect of a baby.' *A grandchild for his parents—what a gift!* 'I know this is completely unexpected. Not in a million years would I have thought... I mean, we were careful.'

'We were. This is so...*unplanned.*'

'But it doesn't follow that it's not a blessing.'

She went still and he chose his next words with care. 'I had to rein in my excitement last night because you deciding not to go ahead with the pregnancy is a valid choice, and an understandable one.'

She sat back and massaged her temples. The conflict he saw mirrored in her face tore at him.

Without a word, she reached out and turned over the first page of the notepad. She'd written a list of pros and cons. Only one item was listed under the 'pros' heading. He read it and something fierce gripped his gut. He didn't bother reading her long list of cons. He seized her hand again. 'If you love this baby, Sarah, then you must keep it.'

Her gaze dropped from his. Her hand trembled. She pulled it free and reached for her tea. 'This baby deserves more than I can give it.'

'We're in this together. I'll help you financially. Between us—' He broke off, his heart thundering in his chest. 'You won't deny me access to the child...will you?'

Her mug clattered back to the table. 'Of course not. I wouldn't dream of it—not if you want to be a part of the baby's life.'

'I want that *very* much.' He wanted them to be very clear on that point.

'But, Majed, I'm not talking about the financial arrangements here. I have—' she rolled her eyes '—marketable skills. I don't doubt my ability to get another job.'

It would be so much harder with a baby, though. And they both knew it.

It took a beat longer for what she wasn't saying

to hit him. He wanted to take her hand again, to offer her silent support, but she had both hands wrapped tightly around her mug. His heart continued to pound. 'Then tell me what you're really afraid of.'

She lifted her gaze and the shadows in her eyes made his stomach clench. 'I think we need to be completely honest with each other from this point forward, if we're going to have a baby together. Don't you?'

There was so much she didn't know about him. And she'd need to know. He resisted the urge to lower his forehead to the table. 'I agree.'

'I need to be honest with you, even if it means you come to despise me.'

For good or ill, his opinion mattered to her. It was why she'd let him think she'd broken up with Superior Sebastian rather than the other way round. He couldn't let her down now. Gently, he reached out to brush the backs of his fingers across her cheek. 'I could never despise you. The idea is unthinkable.'

She took his hand and squeezed it before releasing it with a smile. 'That was the right thing to say.'

Everything inside him sharpened. He sat back with folded arms, his hand still warm from where he'd touched her. 'Now, if I can only get you to believe it. Come, tell me what you're afraid of.'

She swallowed and her throat bobbed. 'Majed, there's a hole inside me—as if there's something essential that I'm missing. And I try to fill it up with things—like my relationship with Sebastian, a relationship I knew wasn't good for me—in an effort to distract myself from that sense of lacking something. It's why I bounce from job to job. Once I start to feel settled in a job, the emptiness starts gnawing away at me. And…and I have to create upheaval to keep it at bay.'

He stared at her. 'Is that why you invited me back to your apartment that night?'

'No, *that* was something I *wanted* to do. I was feeling jubilant and happy and it felt right.' She met his gaze. 'The night I spent with you, I wasn't thinking about filling up any kind of shortfall or lack inside me. I wasn't trying to distract myself. I'm not sure I was thinking at all. I acted on impulse, yes, but on instinct too.' Her frown deepened. 'I felt as if I was living—as if I were properly alive. It was…exhilarating.'

It merely meant she hadn't had time to become bored with him yet. 'And you're afraid that a baby won't be a big enough distraction? You think you'll find yourself becoming bored with the baby, the way you do with your jobs?'

Shocked eyes met his. 'That's *not* what I mean at all. No. I'm afraid that I'll make the baby the very centre of my life—that I'll use it to fill all those empty places inside me. That'd be wrong. It wouldn't be fair to put that kind of pressure on a child. I have a feeling it would be *shockingly* unfair.'

Her honesty stunned him.

The care she was already taking for her child humbled him.

He had empty places inside him too, but he knew exactly what had caused them—the guilt and responsibility he bore over his brother's death. How did he mean to protect a child from those?

'You sense it in me too, don't you?'

'No.' He shook his head. 'You don't appear to me as if some essential part of you is missing. You don't strike me as lonely, or even as if you're afraid of loneliness.' She had a wide network of friends. He'd seen her with them in the bar. From the outside, Sarah's life seemed full. 'Before Sebastian, you were nearly a year without a boyfriend, yes? You don't strike me as a person who needs to constantly be in a romantic relationship to feel whole.'

'The emptiness has nothing to do with romance or loneliness. If it did, I'd be able to fill it.'

'What does it have to do with, then?'

She shrugged but her gaze slid away. Instinct told him not to push. 'Sarah, you don't strike me as someone who is lacking. You strike me as someone who is searching.'

She swung back to gaze at him. 'Searching for what?'

'I expect you're the only person who can answer that.' Though he'd do anything he could to help her find the answer.

She scrubbed her hands down her face. 'I don't want my...*lack*...to hurt the baby.'

'If we're both aware of it as a potential problem then we can remain on our guards against it—cut it off at the pass, so to speak.'

She bit her lip but it didn't hide the hope that flared briefly in her eyes. 'You make it sound easy.'

'I don't think it'll be easy. I think raising a child must be the most challenging thing a person can ever do in this life. I think it must also be one of the most rewarding.'

She sagged back in her chair. 'You make me believe that I could do it.'

She could do it! And how much he wanted to do it too—with her—should scare him. Instead, it elated him.

She pointed at his list. 'Which of these options is the most attractive to you?'

His heart thundered so loud it was all he could do to hear his thoughts over it.

She tapped a finger to the notepad. 'Do you have a...for the lack of a better term...*favourite* here?'

'Yes.' She'd just been completely honest with him. She deserved the same in return.

'Okay,' she whispered. 'Hit me with it.'

'You want the truth? Right now?'

She moistened her lips. 'What are *you* afraid of?'

'Terrifying you.'

After a beat, she started to laugh. 'Being pregnant terrifies me. Wondering whether I'll be a good mother or not terrifies me. But, Majed, *you* don't terrify me.'

Without another word, he pointed to the last item on the list. 'This is my preference.'

Her quick intake of breath told him she hadn't expected that.

'You want us to marry?' she whispered. 'You want to marry me and take me and the baby to live in Keddah Jaleel with you?'

'Yes.' The word croaked out of him. 'Have I terrified you?'

'Umm…no.'

He didn't believe her. But nevertheless it was time to tell her the truth. 'Sarah, there's something you need to know about me. My father is the ruling Sheikh of Keddah Jaleel…and I'm his heir.'

Her face remained blank for a disconcertingly long time before she straightened. 'You…you mean that you're…like a king?'

'My father is the king.'

'But you'll be king one day?'

Acid burned the back of his throat. 'Yes.' *Maybe.*

'And if we marry, and our child is a boy, he'll one day be king too?'

He had to force his answer out. 'Yes.'

She folded her arms tightly in front of her. 'Okay, you can now colour me terrified.'

CHAPTER THREE

SARAH WASN'T SURE at what point she stopped listening. Majed's rich tones continued to wash over her but her mind whirled in a million different directions. He was the son of a king. *He was a prince!* And then one of his statements cut through all her confusion, crystallising into an overarching and urgent question.

'Whoa, wait!' She held up a hand. 'You were sent away from Keddah Jaleel *for your own safety*? Because of border infractions and rebel activity?'

He dragged a hand down his face and she hated how grey he'd gone. 'Majed?'

'Yes.'

'And yet this is a place you want to take me? You're prepared to put your unborn child in danger?'

'No!' His head shot up and his eyes flashed. 'I would never knowingly place you or our child in danger. The skirmishes were minor and quickly smothered, the perpetrators dealt with. It wasn't necessary that I leave, but it put my parents' minds at rest.'

Her heart thumped so hard she swore it would leave bruises. 'Then why have you stayed away from your homeland for the last four years?'

He shot out of his seat to stalk across the room. 'That is not something which I wish to discuss. You have my word of honour, though, that is has nothing to do with fearing for my safety.'

He wanted her to take his word for it? Maybe, if it were only her life at stake here, she would. But it wasn't. She had a baby to consider. She could no longer afford to be reckless or irresponsible.

Rising, she ran her hands over her blouse in a vain effort to smooth out the wrinkles. 'I think it's time I went home.'

Her apartment—Mike's apartment—was only a couple of blocks away. A walk in the early-morning air might help.

Or not. Probably not. But it wouldn't hurt.

His nostrils flared. 'You'll consider my proposal?'

'No.'

Not a single muscle moved and yet he seemed to sag. 'You think the idea too outrageous?'

It was utterly preposterous, yet it wasn't outrage that gripped her. 'I'm not going anywhere near Keddah Jaleel when I've no idea why you've stayed away so long. I know no one there. You'd be my only friend and support, and if I can't trust you...'

Her stomach churned. 'I am not putting myself in that position, Majed. My mother taught me better than that.'

He swung away to pace the length of the room before swinging back to face her. Agitation—anger, perhaps?—crackled from him like a force field. 'An Internet search will provide you with everything you need to know.'

She located her purse and slung it over her shoulder as she made for the door. 'Goodbye, Majed.'

'That is not enough for you?'

She swung back. 'I'm surprised you even need to ask that question. We're going to have a baby and yet you can't be honest with me.' Her hands clenched. 'If you can't see the problem with that, then I'm not going to try and explain it to you.'

His nostrils flared. His chest rose and fell. And for a moment he looked so forbidding, her mouth went dry. He'd never hurt her, she knew that, but she could suddenly see the legacy of his heritage—the fierce and fearless warriors who'd fought and won innumerable wars on the ancient sands of Keddah Jaleel. Their blood flowed in his veins and, beneath his veneer of polish, that same fierceness resided in Majed's DNA.

'You're going to do it. You're going to keep the baby.'

His words were more statement than question. He smiled and she felt as if she were falling. She opened her mouth and then closed it again, realising that she'd come to a decision in spite of herself. Her heart beat hard. She and Majed would be tied to each other always through this child. And, regardless of what happened between them, the thought of the baby could still make him smile. And that mattered.

She rubbed a hand across her chest, trying to dislodge the ache attempting to settle beneath her breastbone. 'I…' She pulled herself up to her full height. 'Yes, I am. I'm going to have this baby.' If nothing else, this morning had made that crystal clear to her.

And that was something to be grateful for.

He strode towards her, and for a moment she thought he meant to hug her, but he stopped short and she saw shadows gathering in his eyes, ousting the excitement and tenderness that had momentarily lit them.

He dragged both hands through his hair. 'Four years ago my brother was killed by the rebels.'

The floor bucked beneath her feet. Sarah braced herself against the door, pressing her spine back until the hard wood bit into her.

'He'd organised a secret assignation with a woman who couldn't be trusted. It was a reckless and foolish thing to do and he paid heavily for it. Too heavily.'

The anguish in his eyes tore at her. 'Oh, Majed.' She reached a hand towards him but he flinched.

'I loved my brother, Sarah. I've not returned to Keddah Jaleel because I cannot imagine living in my homeland without him.'

She wanted to hug him but everything in his posture forbade it. 'I'm sorry,' she whispered.

He nodded, but all she could see in his face was pain and anger. Her stomach churned in a sickening slow roll. *Oh, no you don't.* This was *not* the time to throw up. Closing her eyes, she rested her head back and concentrated on her breathing.

'Come, Sarah.'

Her eyes sprang open at the touch of warm fingers against her arm.

'Come take a seat on the sofa.'

She couldn't fight the nausea and talk at the same time so she let him lead her across to the plump comfort of the sofa. Once seated, she shoved her head between her knees, murmuring, 'I'll be right as rain in a moment.'

When she was finally sure she'd mastered the nausea, she lifted her head. 'I'm sorry about that. I—'

'I shouldn't have told you in such a way!'

'I'm glad you did tell me.'

'Has it made you more afraid to journey to Keddah Jaleel?'

'Not more afraid, just sadder.' And to her surprise she realised she spoke the truth. 'Your brother...'

'Ahmed.'

She swallowed. 'Did Ahmed not follow proper security protocols? I assume you have security measures in place?'

He nodded. 'It's necessary for any ruling family. But that night Ahmed gave his bodyguard the slip.'

Nobody deserved to pay such a high price for wanting a single night of freedom.

'Why did they kill him?' she whispered. 'What did they hope to achieve?'

'My father is a progressive monarch. At some future point, he'd dearly love to introduce democracy to Keddah Jaleel. There are still those in my country, however, who cling to the old ways.'

'Progressive? Is he working towards gender equality? Will, for example, the daughters of the ruling sheikh ever be allowed to rule?'

For the first time that morning, he smiled—really smiled. 'Ah, Sarah, we're progressive...and we'll continue to work towards a fair and just world for all of our citizens...but change cannot always be introduced as quickly we would like.'

'Meaning?'

'Progress takes time. And we must be seen to respect the traditions of our people, even as we move beyond them. If they believe us to view our heritage as worthless, then we would lose their trust and loyalty. If our child is a daughter, and if she shows an interest in politics, then she'll have some kind of leadership role.'

'But she won't be ruler?'

'I cannot see that happening for the next generation, no. But, if we have a granddaughter, things may be different for her.'

She stared at him and her heart thumped. What a difficult task it must be to lead a country. This man was a prince—one day a ruler by birthright. She had no right telling him what he should and shouldn't do politically, not when she had no notion of what his people held dear, what they valued and what they hoped for.

She swallowed. 'Your family have paid a heavy price for their service to your country, Majed. I'm more sorry than I can say about the loss of your brother.'

This time when she reached out to touch his hand he didn't flinch. Instead, he turned his palm upwards and laced his fingers though hers. The scent of amber and spices—cloves and cardamom—teased her senses as a thick, pregnant silence wrapped about them. It was all she could do not to chafe the gooseflesh that rose on her arms.

'There is one other thing you need to know.'

His tone lifted the tiny hairs at her nape.

'Ahmed was my *older* brother.'

'Do you have any other siblings?'

He shook his head and that was when she realised what he was trying to tell her. 'Oh!' Her heart started to thump. 'You… Ahmed was supposed to ascend to the throne, not you?'

'Not me,' he agreed.

Wow! Okay. 'And…and that's another reason you haven't wanted to return?'

'Yes.'

And yet he was prepared to face his demons because he had a baby on the way—because he wanted to be a good father. 'I think you'll make a fine ruler, Majed. I know you must miss Ahmed, but you haven't usurped him.'

'I know that in my head. But it's not the way it feels in my heart.'

'What would Ahmed tell you to do?'

He spoke a phrase in Arabic that she didn't understand. But then he laughed and he suddenly looked younger. 'He'd tell me to stop over-thinking things. He'd tell me I need to curb my impatience for change and to tread with respect in relation to the traditional ways.' A sigh shuddered from him. 'He'd tell me to take my place at my father's side. He'd want me to fight for it.'

Fight for it…?

She wasn't sure what that last bit meant but, as she stared into his face, she couldn't agree more with Ahmed's advice. Majed was destined for great things. It was time for him to embrace his destiny.

'Will you come to Keddah Jaleel with me, Sarah? Will you at least come and see the life you could have there, the life I can give you and our child?'

'What will your parents think about a baby?'

'It will…' The lines about his mouth deepened. 'It will bring them joy.'

She had a feeling that there were family issues at play here that she had no hope of understanding.

'Our unmarried status will not thrill them. It will…disappoint them. But if you find you like Keddah Jaleel then maybe you will stay.'

'And marry you?'

'That is my wish.'

'And what kind of marriage do you think we can have?'

'One based on respect and honesty. One based on friendship.'

She pulled in a breath. 'What about love?'

He dragged his hand from hers. She immediately missed the warmth and connection. He pushed that hand back through his hair once… twice. 'We said we would be honest, yes?'

She couldn't speak. She could only nod. He was going to tell her that he could never love her… and she didn't know why, but she wasn't sure she could bear to hear him say it.

'I do not believe in love.'

She blinked.

'And if I did, I'd not want it in my life.'

What on earth…? So it wasn't that he *couldn't* love her *in particular*. It was that he *wouldn't* love any woman at all.

'Love—romantic love—leads people to do wild and foolish things. It clouds their judgement. I want no part of that.'

Her mouth went dry. He was talking about Ahmed and the woman who had entranced him so completely that he'd thrown caution to the wind.

Oh, Majed.

'I can sincerely assure you, however, that I believe my happiness in marriage with you has a better chance than with anyone else I know. I *like* you, Sarah, and that has to count for something.'

He said that now. But what would happen when he met a woman who stirred his blood? How much would he resent the ties that bound him then—and the woman and child responsible for those ties? Would he become like her father? Would she become like her mother?

She couldn't let that happen.

She moistened parched lips. 'Do you believe in fidelity?'

His eyes flashed. 'I do.' He took her chin in a firm grip and forced her gaze to his. 'I can assure you that, if you marry me, you will not think of other men.'

And then his lips slammed to hers with a force that was far from polite and more demanding than any kiss she'd ever experienced. One hand slid to her nape to prevent her from drawing away, while the other remained at her jaw, holding her still while he plundered her lips with a ruthless and seductive intent that had her melting even as she wanted to resist. The relentless, primal possession continued, sending the blood stampeding through her veins while the strength leached from her muscles until it finally tore his name from her throat.

He lifted his head, his eyes glittering. 'Are we clear on this point?'

She lifted fingers that trembled to swollen lips.

That kiss had been an outrageous attempt at domination, yet she wanted him to kiss her like that again...and not stop.

'I'm clear on the fact that you expect fidelity from me. Do you demand it of yourself?'

'Naturally.' His chin tilted at an arrogant angle. 'But then, I expect my future wife to make sure my mind does not stray to other women.'

She tossed her head, dislodging his grip, thrilled and appalled in equal measure. But before she could give him the put down she was sure he deserved, his lips were on hers again—warm, gentle...playful. They teased and tantalised until her anger had dissolved and she threaded her fingers through his hair to pull him closer.

He obliged until she lay half-sprawled beneath him, their only barrier the thin material of their clothes, his kisses sending something inside her spiralling free. She wanted all barriers between them gone. She wanted to move to the dance he'd taught her six weeks ago. She craved the spiralling pleasure, the adventure of it all, and the peace that followed. She ached...

A whimper broke from her when he lifted his

head. He muttered words she didn't understand but could translate all too easily.

There'd be no more kisses today.

He lifted himself away from her and then helped her back into a sitting position with a gentleness that had the backs of her eyes burning.

'I'm sorry.'

He physically removed himself from the sofa, his words emerging clipped and short. If she hadn't heard the regret threading through them, she might've fled in mortification.

'I'm only sorry you stopped.' She'd aimed for levity but fell far short of the desired mark. It was the truth of her words that rang in the space between them rather than humour. What the heck, she'd made a fool of herself over lesser things. 'Why did you stop?'

He moved to sit in an armchair. She'd love to flatter herself that it was because he couldn't trust his control when he was near her, but she wasn't that kind of woman. She didn't inspire that kind of passion in men.

'I don't want to do anything to make you resent me.'

'And...sex can be complicated?'

'That is my experience, yes.'

Hers too, but she and Majed had already been lovers, they were having a baby—he wanted to marry her, for heaven's sake! Surely...?

'From here on, Sarah, it has to be all or nothing. I won't settle for anything less.'

She gulped.

'As the mother of my future child, you're entitled to my respect and consideration.'

Uh huh.

'I don't want... I should hate to come to resent you. We may marry or not—whatever you decide—but I think it important that we do our very best to maintain our friendship.'

'Absolutely.' Desire continued to shift through her in an insistent ache, an itch and prickle in her blood, but she forced herself to focus on his words. Friendship was important. She remembered what it had been like growing up with warring parents. She'd do anything to protect her child from that. But... 'If you don't believe in love, Majed, why should you come to resent me if we became lovers? I don't understand.'

'I have my pride, *habibi*. Just like any man.'

She was starting to suspect he might have more than his fair share. 'Meaning that, if we became lovers and I then chose not to marry you, that would hurt your pride?'

'Deeply.'

Wow. Okay. He really did mean all or nothing. And she had no intention of rousing his resentment. He could think what he liked of her but she had to make sure he never resented their child.

'I'd resent being the tool with which you recovered from a broken heart.'

Her jaw dropped. 'Broken heart? You mean… Sebastian? Oh, *please*! He didn't break—'

'We promised to be honest with each other.' His lips twisted. 'Do not lie to me now.'

Her hands clenched. 'Sebastian did not break my heart!'

She glared at him but Majed's face had gone opaque. 'Perhaps that is what you want to believe. Perhaps that's what you wish were true.'

She shot to her feet. 'That's the kind of privileged-male superiority that seriously ticks me off! Oh, the poor little woman can't possibly know her own mind—she's just a hysterical female! I'll tell her what she really thinks because she's not clever enough to think for herself.'

The lines bracketing his mouth turned white. He shot to his feet too. 'That's not what I meant.'

'It's what you said.'

He raised his arms. 'You want me to believe Sebastian didn't break your heart?'

'Your belief is your own affair. Just...just don't presume to know my thoughts and feelings better than I do myself.'

They were both breathing heavily. Eventually he nodded. 'You are right. That was wrong of me...and stupid. I resent Sebastian—I resent the way he treated you. The only possible explanation I could come up with for why you accepted that treatment was because you were in love with him.'

'There are other reasons.'

'Such as?'

She fell back into the sofa. 'Do we need to talk about this now? There're a whole lifetime of reasons and it makes me tired and ashamed to think of them.'

He sat again too, his eyes dark and intense as they scanned her face. It suddenly occurred to her that maybe he found her just as baffling as she found him. It comforted her a little, but his continuing seriousness made her fidgety. She shot him a smile. 'Perhaps you'll understand if you ever meet my mother.'

'I want to meet your mother.'

That made her laugh, though not in a particularly humorous way.

'Why do you laugh?'

'My mother will try and eat you for breakfast.'

'Meaning?'

'She subscribes to a particularly militant brand of feminism.'

'And you don't?'

'I'm a feminist—don't doubt that for a moment. I believe in equal rights for women, in equal pay and in equal opportunities. I also believe men can be feminists.'

'But your mother doesn't?'

She shook her head. 'She thinks I'm deluded.'

He rubbed his nape. 'I'm the son of the ruling sheikh in a patriarchal society. She's going to hate me.'

She grimaced. 'Pretty much.'

'I see. It won't be a comfortable meeting, then.' He lifted his chin and met her gaze squarely. 'I still want to meet her.'

Brave man.

'And then I want to meet your father.'

'I suspect that'll be impossible. At least, in the

short-term. He's in America at the moment. But we can call him if you like.'

'Yes. It's necessary.' For a moment a silence stretched and then he said, 'After that…will you come to Keddah Jaleel and meet *my* family? Will you come and see the life you could have there?'

Her heart started to thump so hard, it was all she could do to breathe. Did she dare?

How can you not? This will be your child's heritage. Whether you stay or not, you owe it to this child at least to experience Keddah Jaleel for yourself.

'Majed…'

He leaned towards her, his face intense and so intent on her that it made her pulse pound in her ears. 'Yes?'

'Do I have your word that, if I want to leave Keddah Jaleel, you and your family won't prevent me?'

He smiled, but it was the saddest smile in the world, and Sarah hated herself for putting it there. 'You've heard horror stories of kidnappings in the Middle East?'

She'd promised him honesty, so she nodded.

He came back to the sofa but he didn't take a seat. Instead, he knelt before her and took her hand in both his own. 'You have my word of honour that you'll be free to leave Keddah Jaleel at any time you choose.' He hauled in a breath that left him pale. 'If you have the baby in Keddah Jaleel and then want to leave, you have my word of honour that you can leave with the child if you wish.'

She saw how much it cost him and she believed him utterly.

'Thank you,' she whispered. 'I...I have something else I want you to promise me.'

'Yes?'

She swallowed. 'If you and I end up hurting each other—I know that's not what either one of us wishes, but this is a situation that has the potential to...matter a lot. And it's unfamiliar territory for us both.'

Midnight eyes bored into hers. 'It doesn't have the *potential* to matter. It already matters a great deal.' He frowned when she remained silent. 'What are you trying to ask of me?'

'I grew up with warring parents, Majed.' She rested a hand on her stomach. 'I don't want that for this child. It would be my worst nightmare.'

His face grew grim. 'I see.'

Her chest clenched. 'I've offended you.'

He shook his head. 'I'm just sorry you had such a difficult childhood.' His gaze met hers, confident, steady and full of belief. 'You and I will never descend to such pettiness.'

How could he be so sure?

'But, if it will set your mind at rest, then you have my word. I will never use this child as a weapon against you. I will always speak of you to this child with respect, whether we are together or not, whether we are friends or not. I promise you this.'

'And I promise it too.'

'No. You need make no such promise. I already know you wouldn't do such a thing.'

She wished she had an iota of his confidence.

'So, Sarah, will you come to Keddah Jaleel with me?'

It was her turn to pull a steadying breath into her lungs. 'Okay, here's what I think we should do.' He allowed her to pull him up to sit beside her, but he refused to relinquish her hand, and she was glad of it. 'We wait until the twelve-week mark in my pregnancy to make sure...' She didn't want to jinx them by saying the words out loud.

Majed nodded. 'Yes, I understand this. You're healthy and young, and I don't envisage that anything will go wrong, but perhaps it would be best to wait.'

She nodded, grateful he'd phrased it so tactfully. 'Then you and I will announce the news to my parents.'

He nodded again.

'And then…and then we go to Keddah Jaleel. Initially for a month.'

'A month?' His eyes flared. 'You'll give me a month?' He lifted her hand to press a kiss to her palm. 'Thank you.'

CHAPTER FOUR

THE ENVELOPE IN Majed's top pocket felt as if it were burning a hole to brand his chest through the thin cotton of his shirt. He glanced at Sarah. Was she ready to go to Keddah Jaleel with him yet?

Three days ago she'd had her twelve-week scan. When she'd asked him if he'd wanted to go with her, he'd said yes with such force it had laid him bare. He dragged a hand down his face. It should've appalled him to reveal such vulnerability but it hadn't. Sarah understood his feelings for this baby. She shared them. She wouldn't toy with his emotions when it came to their child. He knew that in his heart. He knew it in his bone marrow. He held tightly to the knowledge.

Her relief at his affirmative answer had laid her bare too, though. She didn't want to do this parenting thing alone. She wanted her baby to know its father. She wanted her baby to know *him*, and the realisation had set something inside him alight.

And then there'd been the moment they'd seen their baby…

The breath jammed in his throat and his heart started to hammer. *His baby!*

He'd been completely unprepared for the rush of love that had gripped him as he'd stared at the image on the monitor. If asked, he'd have said he already loved this child, and had from the moment Sarah had told him about it, but actually to see the baby…hear its heartbeat…

His hands clenched and unclenched. He'd been ridiculously nervous beforehand. He had no idea why. He wasn't prone to histrionics. He didn't have a predilection for envisioning gloomy outcomes. Sarah was young and the picture of health. There was absolutely no reason why she and the baby should be anything but hale and hearty.

But those moments before the monitor had been turned towards them had felt like an eternity. His heart had lodged in his throat, making his lungs ache with the effort to keep breathing. They ached again now at the memory.

Sarah had felt it too. She'd reached for his hand and had squeezed it with all of her might. He'd understood her fear and he hadn't let go of her hand again until the scan was complete. She'd needed his strength and he meant to give her whatever she needed.

And then the technician had turned the monitor towards them and Sarah's grip had changed—strong, still, but charged with relief...and with awe and excitement. In that instant he hadn't known what was more beautiful—the child on the screen or the love that unfurled across Sarah's face in a warm, golden glow as elemental and awe-inspiring as a sunrise. It had stolen his breath. It had made him ache.

And then she'd met his gaze and her smile had been so big and so *real* that all the breath had flowed back into his body. Her smile had included him so completely and utterly that he hadn't been able to resist it. It had said, *this is our child. Look what we've made. Isn't it beautiful?*

Suddenly they weren't two people thrown together in difficult circumstances trying to work out the best way forward, but two people looking at the life they'd created. In that moment the shadowy, insubstantial bond they shared had crystallised, cementing them together. No matter what happened in the future, they were parents of this child. And they were determined to do whatever was best for it, regardless of the expense to themselves.

He glanced across at her again. They'd taken to spending Monday nights together—dinner out at one of the many local restaurants followed by coffee and conversation, or sometimes a movie back at Sarah's apartment. They always sat— or sprawled—on adjacent sofas, careful not to touch. Sarah dropped into the bar several times a week—just like she used to—but somehow they'd not managed to recapture their old camaraderie.

Because you slept with her. And you want to sleep with her again.

He didn't just *want* it—he *ached* with it. It plagued his dreams at night. It teased and tormented him. But...

He lifted his chin. He refused to allow passion to cloud his judgement or sway his decisions. He'd been blindsided by desire and lust before and it had cost his brother his life. He would *not* let that happen again.

He stared at his hand. The memory of the way she'd gripped it during the scan rose again in his mind. Sarah wanted what was best for this child.

With a deep breath, he pulled the envelope from his pocket and slid it across to her.

'What's this?' With a glance at him, she took it…and then stilled. He watched the bob of her throat as she swallowed and a familiar thirst rose through him. The friendship they'd been trying to establish for the last seven weeks did nothing to cool the stampede of heat in his blood, or dispel the ache that gripped him when he gazed at the plump promise of her bottom lip. He craved to suck that lip into his mouth, bite down gently on it, before laving it with his tongue. He…

'These are tickets to Keddah Jaleel.'

He pulled his mind back from X-rated visions of Sarah naked, to find her staring at him with wide eyes. Perspiration prickled his top lip. 'Are you really surprised?'

'I… Well, I guess I shouldn't be.'

But she was. Maybe he should've led up to this more gently. 'The date is open-ended. You, of course, get to decide when we fly out.'

'Have…have you organised a replacement manager for the bar?'

He nodded. His second-in-command was ready to step up to the job whenever Majed asked it of him. He'd spoken to Mike, and Mike had no objections.

Sarah bit her lip as she stared at their tickets. He understood her anxiety, but her vulnerability caught at him. Although they were constantly careful not to touch—other than that isolated incident during the scan—he was tempted to move across to her sofa and take her in his arms. His pulse quickened. *Don't be an idiot.* 'What are you worried about?'

'That your family will hate me.'

'They won't hate you. That'd be impossible.'

'But they might disapprove of me. They might be disappointed in us both.'

'If they are, they'll be too polite to say so in front of you.'

She managed a short laugh. 'I wish I could promise you the same good manners from my mother.'

This child would go a long way to healing his parents' hearts. He longed to alleviate their pain. Nothing and no one could ever replace Ahmed in their lives, and his father might never be able to look at Majed in the same way again—not since the details surrounding Ahmed's death had emerged—but he'd dote on a grandchild. It seemed the least Majed could do. In time, his father might even find a way to forgive him.

But what if Sarah didn't want to stay?

The thought burned a path of acid through him. His hands clenched. He'd have to return to Australia with her, turn his back on Keddah Jaleel and any hope of becoming his father's heir…and on any hope there might be a way he and his father could repair their relationship. Darkness—thick and black—tried to settle over him. He did what he could to beat it back. He'd do what he needed to do. His child's wellbeing and happiness came before all else.

He lifted his head, recalling the way Sarah had gripped his hand during the scan and the deep love that had transformed her as she'd stared at the image of their baby. A deep-seated recognition coursed through him. Like him, Sarah would do what was right for this baby, regardless of the personal cost to herself. She wanted her baby surrounded by love. She'd never deny it a father who loved it, a father who wanted to be an integral part of its life.

He pushed his shoulders back and found he had to fight a fierce smile. He could offer this baby and her a life of unparalleled luxury and opportunity. For their child's sake she wouldn't be able to turn her back on all that Majed could provide—the privileged life he could offer their child—even if she cared nothing for such things for herself.

She'd come to the same conclusion once she'd been to Keddah Jaleel and had fallen in love with his family, his country and his people. Her loyalty to her child would win out. But with Sarah a gently-gently, softly-softly approach would be best. He had no desire to force her hand. She needed to feel that she'd made the decision herself, that she hadn't been led…that she was free from pressure and expectation. She needed to come to the conclusion in her own time, not his. And he'd do everything in his power to facilitate that.

He loved this child. He wanted to be a part of its life. She knew that and it meant something to her. She'd do the right thing.

Sarah scrolled through the calendar on her tablet. 'I only need to give the temp agency a week's notice. So…' She shuffled to the end of her sofa nearest to him and he moved to the end nearest to her. 'What if we have dinner with my mother this coming Saturday night…? And we can talk to my father that evening too. And then…and then we could fly out to Keddah Jaleel on the following Saturday? It should give us ample time to get ourselves organised.'

'Perfect. I'll let my parents know to expect us then.'

'Are you going to tell them about the baby?'

'We'll do that together once we arrive—face to face.'

Her smile trembled and he broke their unspoken no-touching rule to reach out and grip her hand. 'It'll be okay, I promise. Just give it a chance.'

'And I thought that you choosing dress-making as a career choice was your greatest mistake!'

Beside Majed, Sarah flinched.

Irene Collins fixed first her daughter and then Majed with a martinet's stare that managed to make him feel he was ten years old again and on the receiving end of a serious scolding from his paternal great-grandmother, who hadn't held with Majed's father's form of parenting. She hadn't been a 'spare the rod' woman. She'd terrified both him and Ahmed.

Irene Collins terrified him in a similar fashion now.

Don't be a coward.

He'd been tutored in the art of diplomacy. He should find this interview—confrontation— relatively easy. Relative, say, to mediating between warring nations, or introducing a new system of government into his homeland, this *should* be a doddle.

But it wasn't.

'Let me see if I have this right,' Irene repeated— she even insisted that Sarah call her Irene. 'Not only are you pregnant, but you're going to *voluntarily* allow this man to escort you to his country *in the Middle East*?'

'His name is Majed, Mother, and I'd appreciate it if you'd maintain some semblance of civility and use it.'

It hadn't taken him long to figure out that, whenever Sarah wanted to annoy Irene, she called her 'Mother'.

'Majed isn't some stranger I picked up in a bar on the spur of the moment and had a random one-night stand with. We've been friends for quite some time. And, whatever else happens, we mean to maintain that friendship. I...' Sarah lifted her chin. 'I insist you treat him with respect.'

Go, Sarah! Something akin to admiration

warmed his chest. In her own way she was just as strong as her mother. He wondered if she realised that.

Irene folded her arms. 'At least you got rid of that ridiculous specimen you were dating previously. What was his name?'

Majed's lip curled. 'Sebastian.'

Irene—her spine ramrod-straight—eyed him from her armchair opposite the sofa where he and Sarah sat. Although she evidently shared Majed's opinion of Superior Sebastian, he couldn't detect an ounce of softening in her gaze. Sarah had told him that Irene was the area manager for a building society. He was simply grateful she wasn't his boss.

He yearned to reach out and take Sarah's hand—offer her support, provide a united front—but she looked as untouchable as her mother. It occurred to him then that she might've kept Sebastian around so long simply to annoy her mother. Childish, undoubtedly, but understandable.

Irene flicked a piece of lint from her trousers. 'Have you spoken to that patriarchal, profiting pillock of a father of yours?'

Majed choked.

'Not yet.'

That seemed to unbend Irene a fraction.

Sarah didn't elaborate further and Majed didn't blame her. They were planning to speak to Sarah's father tonight. He started to see why she'd made him promise never to let their child become caught in a tug-of-war battle between them. His heart ached for the young Sarah who'd had to suffer through all of that.

'I take it you're well?'

'Very. I've had a little morning sickness, but that seems to have passed. The baby is due in October.'

Irene stuck out her chin. 'You know my feelings on men.'

Sarah glanced at Majed. 'Irene doesn't believe a man is necessary to a woman's happiness.'

He met Irene's gaze. 'You don't believe in love?'

'Romantic love? No.' Her raised eyebrow challenged him. 'Do you?'

He believed in it. He just didn't want it. 'My parents have a very successful marriage, but their union was arranged by their families. It has made me see that love is not a necessary component for a successful marriage. I believe mutual respect, shared values and friendship are far more important—and will bring more long-term happiness to one's life. My parents value and respect each other deeply.'

Love could be such a fleeting emotion—an emotion that in his experience was worth neither the heartache nor the upheaval. 'They have been wonderful role models. My childhood was very happy.'

'And are *they* happy?'

His gut clenched. He could feel his face turn wooden. 'Several years ago my brother died. They have had a difficult time since then.' How did one learn to accept the unacceptable, adjust to the un-adjustable?

Irene sat back a fraction, an almost imperceptible sigh infinitesimally loosening her shoulders. Sarah leaned forward, as if sensing that Majed needed a moment's respite—a moment to re-gather his resources. For the last four years he'd managed to avoid any mention of Ahmed, but in the last few weeks he'd been forced to acknowledge his brother's death. And each time it felt as if a sword were slashing his vitals.

'There's more you should know.'

'Dear God, don't tell me you're considering marrying this man, Sarah? Don't be such a little fool! It's completely unnecessary. I'll make sure you're looked after, that you have everything you need—you and the baby.'

Irene's unswerving show of support comforted a part of him that he hadn't known needed comforting. Irene might be tough and uncompromising but she loved her daughter.

'You cannot be serious!' Irene shot to the edge of her chair when Sarah remained silent. 'I raised you with more street smarts than that!'

'That's my own concern.' Sarah stuck out her chin. 'I haven't made a decision yet. The *more* you need to know is that Majed's father is the ruling Sheikh of Keddah Jaleel and that...'

She gripped her hands together, her white knuckles betraying her nervousness.

'Majed is his heir.'

Majed *should* be his heir, Majed corrected silently. If his father disowned him completely then that would change. It was too difficult to try and explain. They'd travel to Keddah Jaleel and he'd discover if he still had a place there.

'I see.' Irene took several agitated turns about the room before resuming her seat. 'What do you know about Keddah Jaleel?'

'I know where it is on the map. I know its climate, its primary industries and the name of its major river.'

She did?

'But I won't pretend that's what you want to know. You mean, what do I know about the politics of the place.' She pressed her hands together. 'Majed's father and uncles are transitioning the country to a democracy with a view to their family becoming a constitutional monarchy—much like Great Britain. At the moment Sheikh Rasheed—Majed's father—is something midway between an absolute ruler and a prime minister.'

'And from where have you had this? From Majed himself?'

Sarah actually laughed. 'For heaven's sake, Mum, you taught me better than that.'

Her 'Mum' sounded far more natural—and affectionate—than her previous 'Irene's or 'Mother's.

Irene's gaze speared to him. 'I assume there's an under-representation of women in both civic and industry leadership roles in your country?'

'Yes, but—'

'No buts! It's appalling.'

'No more appalling than it is in this country.'

It took an effort to keep his voice level. 'It's an issue my father is working hard to address, but this kind of change doesn't happen overnight. Currently we're making more university places available to women.' He straightened. 'We intend to have the best educated female population in the world.'

'Which will do them no good if they're not allowed to use their education to better their own situations.'

'That will come.' He found himself on his feet, his fierce love for his country and his people rising through him. 'Tell me what it is that you really fear. Why are you worried about Sarah's visit to Keddah Jaleel?'

Irene stood too. She stabbed a finger at his chest. 'I'm *worried* that once you get her there she'll be a virtual prisoner. I'm *worried* that you and your family will compromise her reproductive autonomy. I'm worried that you'll take the child and that if Sarah proves troublesome—and, believe me, my daughter knows how to be troublesome—you'll imprison her...or worse.'

He swore softly in his native tongue. 'Madam, I am not a barbarian. Nor are my family or my fellow countrymen. Sarah—and her child—will be free to come and go as and when they choose. It's true that I hope Sarah will marry me but I would never force her.'

'A marriage that will be more to your benefit than hers.'

'A marriage that will be *mutually* beneficial.'

'Mum!' Sarah hissed. Grabbing Majed's arm, she tugged him back down to the sofa beside her. 'I'm going to visit Keddah Jaleel for a month but I've made no decision beyond that.'

Irene smoothed a hand down her trousers and sat. 'It occurs to me that the wife of the ruling sheikh could do a lot of good in Keddah Jaleel.'

No doubt she meant in relation to women's rights. It occurred to him that he hadn't really considered the political implications of marrying Sarah. All he'd thought about was how a grandchild would help to heal his parents' hearts. Marrying Sarah could be the final nail in the coffin of Majed's hope to work alongside his father for his country's betterment.

Would his countrymen accept Sarah?

He pushed his shoulders back. If Sarah accepted his proposal of marriage then they'd have to. Somehow he'd make it work.

* * *

They hung up from the call they'd just had with Sarah's father, and for a moment Majed didn't know what to say.

'I did warn you,' Sarah said.

Dear God, she'd had to grow up with these people? His heart ached at the thought of the young girl she must've been, and all she must've suffered being at the centre of the tug-of-war between two such embittered people—people who'd once claimed to love each other.

'He liked you,' she offered.

'Only after discovering your mother didn't approve of me.' He'd actually called Irene a 'ball-busting old witch'. 'He didn't even congratulate you on the baby.' He'd just gone off into ugly torrents of laughter when he'd imagined the look on Irene's face as she'd heard their news.

'He offered me money instead.'

He knew people showed their love in different ways, but…

He shoved his shoulders back. Nobody in Keddah Jaleel would treat Sarah with unkindness or disrespect; he wouldn't let anyone turn her into a pawn in a game. He'd make sure of it.

He made his smile gentle, calm…encouraging. 'Are you ready to come to Keddah Jaleel now?'

She gave a half-laugh that tightened his chest. 'Yes, it's time for me to face the dragons on your side of the fence.'

'No dragons,' he promised. At least, not for her. He'd draw all their fire on himself if need be. It was the least that he could do.

CHAPTER FIVE

'NO! YOU'RE JOKING!'

Sarah stopped dead on the tarmac to stare at him, and he had to swallow back a laugh. 'No joke,' he assured her.

Her eyes widened even further. 'You have your own private jet?'

'It belongs to my country, not to me or my father personally.' But his father *had* very thoughtfully provided it for them. That had to be a good sign.

'So, what you're telling me is that we're travelling in that?'

She pointed at the sleek jet gleaming in the mid-morning sun and he nodded. 'Lovely, isn't it?' With a laugh, he took her arm. 'Wait until you see inside. It's amazing. Mind your step. The stairs are steep.'

He waved the flight attendant away and buckled Sarah into an armchair-sized seat himself, taking delight in her simple astonishment and growing awe. *It's for the plane, remember, not for you.*

He buckled himself into the seat beside her. 'What do you think?'

She ran her hand over the cream leather of the seats and pulled her feet from her sandals to dig her toes into the plush carpet. 'I understand textiles are a big industry in Keddah Jaleel.'

'We're proud of our textile industry—justifiably so. We have some of the finest artisans in the Middle East. We make exquisite carpets, beautiful silks and the finest cottons. Only the best materials and most skilled workers were employed for the kitting out of the jet.' He glanced at the stewardess standing nearby. 'Even the flight attendants' uniforms have been made locally. Would you like a pre-flight drink?'

Sarah ordered a lemonade and then pointed with a shy smile at the stewardess's scarf. 'That is truly lovely.'

The stewardess returned with glasses of lemonade and sparkling mineral water, as well as a complimentary scarf for Sarah, who went into immediate raptures over it. Her cheeks grew pink when she became aware of Majed's scrutiny. 'I'm sorry.'

'Don't apologise. I'm pleased it finds favour with you.'

'I dreamed of being a designer…once upon a time.'

He recalled Irene's scathing, *'And I thought you choosing dress-making as a career was your greatest mistake!'* He remembered the way Sarah had flinched.

'I soon wised up on that front, but I still have a passion for fabric and cloth.'

He fought back a frown. 'What do you mean, wised up? Why did you not pursue this passion?'

She rolled her eyes. 'Because passion doesn't always translate to talent. One needs more than enthusiasm.' She shuffled upright in her seat and touched her glass to his. 'To a good flight.' She sipped and then let out an exaggerated sigh. 'Real crystal?'

He nodded. 'Real crystal.'

'This is how you live in Keddah Jaleel?'

He tried to see the luxury through her eyes. He hadn't missed it, but maybe he'd taken it for granted. 'The economy of Keddah Jaleel is flourishing. It allows the Sheikh a great deal of…'

'Opulence? Luxury? Splendour?'

'Comfort,' he countered. 'You have to understand that a display of this kind of statesmanship is designed to impress, to give a sense of largesse, to showcase the country's prosperity.'

'Is that another way of saying "to show off"?'

He chuckled. There was something about Sarah that made him feel young. That made it easy to laugh. 'I see I'm going to have to teach you the art of diplomacy.'

Despite her teasing, though, he could see that the jet, the luxury and the respect afforded him from the flight crew impressed her. And he meant to push every advantage he had at his disposal. 'We're very fortunate to be able to enjoy such a lifestyle. If you choose to, Sarah, you can enjoy all of this too.'

Rather than wriggling with excitement, or staring at him with wide eyes, her gaze slid away and she sipped her drink, rubbing her free hand across her chest as if to ease an ache. He'd read that pregnant women often suffered from heartburn. 'Do you feel unwell?'

'I'm fine.' She turned back with a smile that didn't quite reach her eyes. 'What did my mother say to you before we left last night?'

He allowed the abrupt change of subject. He didn't doubt that it had been preying on her mind.

'She told me that she had a lot of resources at her disposal—that she knows important people—and if I thought I could hold you against your will then I had another thing coming.'

She winced. 'I'm sorry.'

'Don't apologise. I don't blame her for her fears, or for doing what she can to ensure your safety.' He sipped his drink before sending her a sidelong look. 'She said that the two of you have a code word...and so I'd better watch myself.'

That got a laugh from her. 'We do.'

He turned to her more fully. 'Really? What is it?'

'My mother taught me better than that, Majed,' she chided, piquing his curiosity further. 'It's a secret—just between her and me. That's the point of it.'

She surveyed him for a moment, head cocked to one side. 'You know, it wouldn't hurt us to have a code word too. Just in case.'

'Just in case of what?' He laughed. 'So I can rescue you if one of my relatives starts to bore you half to death or...?'

'Oh, no! A code word isn't to be used for trivial things, but only in the direst of circumstances. If one of us utters it, or writes it down, or somehow or other telegraphs it to the other, then it means they're in terrible trouble and to get help. We're talking big help here, Majed—like the police.'

He stiffened. 'I'll let no harm come to you in Keddah Jaleel, Sarah. I swear. Are you frightened?'

'I'm nervous about meeting your parents. I'm not frightened for my life or my freedom. But it's a fact of life that people—women—are murdered every day. Random events happen. It never hurts to have a code word.'

He supposed not. But the thought of Sarah needing one disturbed him. He didn't want his perturbation to worry her, so he forced himself to smile. 'You're right. It won't hurt.' *And if it'll put her mind at rest...*

He turned back to find her staring at his mouth, as if totally mesmerised. On cue, a roaring hunger surged through him. She could take him from laughing, to perplexed, to arousal in less than three beats of his heart. She shook herself, her cheeks turning pink. 'You and your father are important men. Don't you have code words with each other...with your bodyguards?'

He couldn't answer for his father but as for him... 'No.'

'Then you should.'

If the future panned out the way he wanted it to, he'd consider it. Until then… 'Let's create one now. It can't be something we'd use in normal conversation?'

'No.'

He stared at her face, at the colour of her lips. 'Coral… Will that suffice, do you think?'

'Coral?' She nodded. 'Perfect.'

If Sarah had been impressed by the deference Majed had been treated to from the moment they'd arrived at the airport in Melbourne, it was nothing to how impressed she was at the pomp and ceremony he received once they'd landed in Keddah Jaleel.

She'd had a brief impression of blazing sands, a glittering ocean and an unexpectedly green belt of land before the plane had descended. She'd turned to Majed and had said stupidly, 'You have beaches!'

The closer they'd got to Keddah Jaleel, the more morose Majed had become. She knew his thoughts must be with Ahmed but she didn't know how to comfort him. She sensed he wouldn't welcome any attempts on her part to intrude into his solitude. He'd been so solicitous towards her, so supportive, that she'd remained quiet and left him to the privacy of his thoughts.

But her words now made him laugh. 'You're surprised, *habibi*?'

Heat curled in her abdomen. She liked it when he called her that. She liked it a little too much. She fought back a frown. 'I shouldn't be, I suppose. I mean, I looked Keddah Jaleel up on the map. I knew it wasn't land-locked.' But beaches hadn't occurred to her.

'My family has a villa on the coast which we sometimes use for vacations. We could spend a few days there, if you would like.'

'That sounds...wonderful.' Australia was renowned for its beaches. It was one of the things she thought she'd miss if she moved to Keddah Jaleel.

If.

Nerves immediately made her stomach churn. Then the plane was on the ground and her entire body turned to jelly. *Please let his family like me.*

Upon landing, Majed's conviviality fled. He became almost grim. She knew he must be going through a hundred different kinds of hell, and she refused to trouble him with her own anxieties—they seemed so paltry in comparison—but...

She slid her hand into his. 'Majed, I know you're thinking about Ahmed and missing him, but this is your home. You have happy memories and associations here too. You're *allowed* to be happy that you're back.' He shouldn't feel guilty about that.

Dark eyes turned to meet her gaze. 'This country is in my blood, and it's leaping to be back here, fired with something more elemental than joy—a recognition that this is where I belong.' His brows drew together, his eyes dark with confusion. 'I didn't expect that.'

Wow. Sarah had never felt that about any place.

'I've stayed away too long.'

He glanced at their linked hands, and a sigh shuddered out of him, and before her eyes he transformed into another man—the same, yet different. He became taller, broader, more serious…and, if it were possible, more tempting. His spine straightened, his jaw lifted and hardened, and determination filled his eyes. She suddenly saw a man who was destined to be king.

It should make her want to flee.

Her heart started to pound as all her mother's dire warnings bombarded her, even as something traitorous softened in her stomach. If she married

Majed, she'd have him in her bed every night. She moistened parched lips.

You can't make such an important, life-altering decision based on hormones.

There was no denying, however, that the thought was an alluring one.

Seductive.

Tempting.

'Sarah!'

Majed's sharp tones snapped her back, and she realised she hadn't been attending to a single word he'd said. She swallowed, and prayed he hadn't deciphered the directions of her thoughts. 'I'm sorry.'

His eyes flashed. 'Never mind—the journey has been a long one.'

She couldn't help thinking that it took all his patience to keep his tone level and gentle. She swallowed again. All her life she'd tried people's patience. Now, it appeared, she'd try Majed's. 'What were you saying?'

His eyes scanned her face before he spoke. 'My parents will receive us at the palace, but there'll be a small reception on the ground here at the airport to welcome me home.'

He undid her seatbelt and helped her to her

feet. She had to lock her knees to keep them from shaking.

'There are protocols it'd be best for you to follow.'

'Such as?'

'Remain a few paces behind me. Don't address me unless I speak to you first.'

She took a step away from him, her stomach rebelling. What had she let herself in for?

His chin shot up. 'Don't look at me like that. I hate this as much as you do, but this is only until we get to the palace. If I take you out there on my arm, like I wish to, we'll have an entire country thinking we're engaged.'

The flight attendant stood waiting patiently in the doorway. Majed turned and snapped a few rapid-fire words at her, and she immediately withdrew, quietly closing the door behind her.

She'd done his bidding, just like that. Without asking questions or demurring or…anything!

It hit her then that Majed would one day be a king. He might not hold the title at the moment, but he'd been bred to rule.

And she…? She was a nobody!

And here he was, advancing on her with a determined light in his eye, and she found herself giving way before him.

'Have you come to a decision yet, *habibi*? Would you perhaps like to be married to the ruling sheikh and live a life of privilege and luxury?'

'Don't be ridiculous.' But her words emerged breathily…huskily….as if she were inviting him to…

The backs of her legs hit the long bench-seat, and she'd have sprawled along its length if Majed hadn't reached out and pulled her against the hard, masculine length of his body.

'You look at me with such hungry eyes that… that I'm tempted to undress you right now—to make love to you until you beg me not to stop.' His hands drifted down to her hips with seductive slowness. 'Until you cry out my name at the pleasure I can give you.'

His fingers curled into the flesh of her hips, sending coursing flames of desire licking through her veins, and she swayed into him. He held her so close, she could feel the hard length of him pressing against her belly. Both their chests rose and fell too quickly.

She tossed her hair and met his gaze. 'If we

make love now, Majed, I can promise you that I won't be the only one crying out my pleasure.'

His nostrils flared, his gaze narrowing in on her lips. 'And afterwards I'd take you out there on my arm.'

She pulled air into lungs that felt as if they were going to burst. 'Then you'd risk looking a fool in the eyes of your countrymen if I decide to not stay in Keddah Jaleel. I'm sorry, Majed, but you can't seduce me into submission.'

'Are you sure about that?' One side of his mouth hooked up in a deliciously wicked grin. 'You bring out the barbarian in me. I find myself tempted to take up your challenge.'

One of his hands travelled from her hip to her armpit, brushing the side of her breast with delicious intent that had her biting her lip as her nipples pebbled into hard nubs that pressed against the thin cotton of her blouse. He stared at them in hunger...and triumph.

Suddenly, she *wasn't* sure, and it frightened her like nothing else had. She wrenched herself out of his arms. 'Positive!'

He stared at her for a moment and then gave a curt nod. 'That's better. You have colour in your face again.'

Her jaw dropped. *He'd...he'd done that on purpose?*

Before she could tell him what she thought of his tactics, he'd turned on his heel and strode out of the plane, leaving her to scrabble her composure into place and scramble after him.

'That was a dirty, rotten trick.' She started the moment the limousine pulled away, the tinted glass shielding them from the crowd's curious gaze, the soundproof barrier between them and the driver securely in place.

'It was, but we were running out of time.' He sent her a sidelong glance. 'But none of it was lies. I'd very much like to...'

'Don't!' She pointed a finger at him. 'Enough of that.'

He took her hand and laced his fingers through hers. 'The fact is, there's a lot at stake here, and appearances are important. I want to shield you as much as I can from unwanted attention and curiosity. For that to happen, you need to be almost invisible—in the same way a brisk, efficient aide would be invisible.'

What he'd done hit her then, and she couldn't help but be grateful for it. If she'd appeared on that welcome committee's red carpet looking nervous…as if she wanted to run…she'd have drawn attention to herself and questions would've been asked. The sense of outrage he'd evoked in her, along with his assured, autocratic arrogance, had protected her from that. Still…

'Couldn't you have just explained all of that to me?' She wasn't stupid. She'd have understood.

'I tried to, but you weren't listening.'

Heat burned her cheeks. She'd been too busy fantasising about Majed to pay attention to anything he'd been trying to tell her. And if she hadn't been such a complete and utter twit she'd have realised there would be protocols it would be best for her to follow.

She was such a flake—a screw-up. What on earth made her think she could successfully move in the same circles as Majed? If he married, he needed an assured diplomat at his side… not someone like her.

'Are you going to be sick?'

His concern tugged at her. 'I'm fine. Just appalled at my own naivety. You better tell me how to address your father and mother, and any other protocols I should be aware of.' Majed had shown her nothing but wholehearted support. The least she could do in return was not embarrass him.

She listened intently as he gave her a quick rundown on palace protocol.

She moistened her lips. 'And what kind of… welcome can I expect from your parents?'

'In public, they'll be very formal, and I expect they'll rarely address you.'

'In private?'

Majed's cheekbones, high and angular, suddenly seemed to stand out in stark relief to the rest of his face. His eyes went pitch-black. Generous lips pressed into a hard line. 'My father is a reserved man. He keeps his true feelings under lock and key.'

Right. She shouldn't expect a warm welcome from him, then. She glanced at Majed out of the corner of her eye. His relationship with his father sounded complicated.

'My mother is the opposite—effervescent and warm. She'll take you under her wing and treat you like a baby chick.'

Her lips twisted. 'Nothing like the welcome you received from my mother, then.'

He laughed, and the hard lines of his face momentarily softened, but he stared out of the window and not at her. 'Look.'

He pointed and she followed the line of his finger. Her jaw dropped.

'The royal palace of Keddah Jaleel.'

On a hill to their right, overlooking the city of Demal—the capital of Keddah Jaleel—stood an enormous palace of white stone and gleaming blue enamel. It had a huge central dome made of silver that gleamed in the sun. There was a cascade of descending half-domes, vaults and ascending buttresses. Numerous slender minarets rose into the sky with a grandeur and grace that left Sarah breathless.

She'd researched Keddah Jaleel's history and geography, its climate and economy. She'd read about Demal's religious diversity and knew that it boasted several mosques, a Catholic cathedral and several Buddhist temples, but she hadn't thought to research its royal palace.

'It's…amazing.'

'We're rather proud of it.'

'It looks like a cross between a fortress and something from the *Arabian Nights*.'

His eyes glowed. 'It has seen a lot of history.'

And then they were gliding through the towering gates and being ushered into the inner sanctum of the palace grounds. An enormous fountain stood in the middle of a generous square that was lined with date palms and drenched with the scent of jasmine and cloves. The water sent a rainbow arcing through the air, fragile and yet beautiful against the fierce blue of the sky. She wasn't sure she'd ever seen anything more beautiful in her life.

She stood to one side and did her best to look deferential, trying to keep her eyes on the ground, rather than darting from side to side to take in all the splendour. Majed held an arm out towards her. 'Come.'

He led her through one of the nearby arches and along a corridor that afforded her glimpses of exotic courtyards and grand rooms.

'We've been lucky to be spared a formal reception.'

She couldn't tell from his tone or his expression whether he considered that a good thing or not.

'Instead we've been summoned to my parents' private apartments.'

Sarah's heart immediately hammered up into her throat. She'd thought she'd have a chance to freshen up before meeting Majed's parents.

He smiled down at her. 'You don't need to be afraid. They're rulers, but they're also people like you and me. Just be yourself.'

Oh, right. She could just imagine them being impressed by a complete and utter flake.

They were halfway across a courtyard—shadier and more beautiful than any other she'd so far seen—when a woman came flying across from the building opposite. 'Majed! Majed, my son!'

The woman flung her arms around Majed and held him tight. Sarah watched them embrace and a lump unexpectedly lodged in her throat. This woman hadn't seen her son in the flesh for four years. Sarah felt like an intruder.

'You must be Sarah?'

She glanced around to find a pair of dark eyes, identical to Majed's, surveying her. 'Your Highness, I...'

She went to curtsey, but he held up his hand. 'You must call me Rasheed.' And to her utter amazement he embraced her, kissing her on both cheeks before holding her close. 'Thank you for bringing my son back home to us, my dear,' he whispered in her ear.

Sarah found herself hugging him back.

CHAPTER SIX

WHEN HIS MOTHER finally loosened her arms from about his neck, Majed turned to greet his father, his insides coiling up tight.

To his surprise, one of his father's hands rested on Sarah's shoulder, and it was evident from the relief in her eyes and the pink in her cheeks that he'd greeted her warmly.

Majed let out a pent-up breath before bowing formally, as was the custom, and when he straightened he found his father's warmth had retreated behind an impenetrable wall of reserve. Even though it was what he expected, it made Majed's gut clench. 'Hello, Father—it's good to see you.'

'Hello, Majed.' He nodded towards Majed's mother. 'It is good to see your mother so happy.'

He felt the sting of the reprimand like a whip against bare flesh. *How could you be so heartless as to make your mother suffer?* He understood immediately what his father hadn't said—that

Majed's presence did not make *him* happy. He'd tolerate his son's presence for his wife's sake and that was all.

Sarah glanced at Majed and his father and back again, her brow crinkling. He didn't blame her for her confusion. Should he have given her a clearer picture of how things stood between him and his father?

In all honesty, he hadn't known if things had changed during his absence, whether his father's attitude had softened…or whether he'd still feel the same way.

His hands clenched. Evidently it was the latter.

Evidently he still held Majed responsible for his brother's death.

And why shouldn't he? Majed still blamed himself. He didn't deserve forgiveness, but there was still the possibility that he could bring some measure of light into his parents' lives.

He gestured Sarah forward. 'Mâmâ, this is my friend, Sarah Collins.'

'Your Highness.'

Sarah curtsied in the fashion of his people and he stared at her in surprise—when had she learned to do that?

'It's a great honour to meet you.' And then she

held her tongue. One did not speak to the Sheikh or Sheikha unless addressed first.

To his further surprise, his mother didn't embrace Sarah. She didn't even offer her hand. She merely said, 'I hope you'll be comfortable during your stay.' And then she turned back to him. 'Majed, you owe your mother a little of your time, surely? Come now to my sitting room. We have so much to catch up on. You must give me time to feast my eyes upon you.'

What on earth...? He glanced back at Sarah.

'The servants will see to your friend.'

Sarah smiled at him and nodded, encouraging him to go, but he sensed the nerves behind that brave little smile—saw the way she pressed her hand to her stomach, as if to protect her child from an unseen force. *His child.* Sarah deserved his consideration. He wouldn't abandon her at the first available opportunity.

'I'm sorry, Omme.' He used the formal term for mother. 'I'd prefer to attend to Sarah myself. Please give us half an hour to freshen up after the flight and we'll meet with you and Abii in his private sitting room.'

'As you wish.'

It was all he could do not to wince at the coldness that threaded his mother's voice or the way she swept from the courtyard. Very few people denied the Sheikha her wishes...except on occasion her sons. She did deserve better from him, but she'd understand once she learned that Sarah was pregnant.

His father's eyes flashed a reprimand in Majed's direction but he touched Sarah's arm in a courtly gesture of leave taking and told her he looked forward to speaking with her more, before he too set off in the same direction as his wife.

When they disappeared from view, Sarah spun to him. 'You should've gone with her, Majed. She's not seen you in four years.'

He glanced meaningfully towards a shady corner where a servant waited patiently. Sarah swallowed and bit her lip, but nodded her understanding—they weren't alone and anything she'd prefer not to be overheard needed to wait. She didn't speak again until the servant had led them to the guest quarters. As Majed had requested, Sarah had been given the best suite of rooms.

The servant melted away at a signal from Majed and Sarah glanced at him with a raised eyebrow. 'Is it okay to speak now?'

'I know you wish to berate me for not going with my mother but, Sarah, my first duty is to you.'

Her face turned wooden. 'Duty?'

He bit back a sigh. 'I didn't mean it that way. I don't see you as a duty. But I promised you every care and consideration while you were here, and I meant it. I've no intention of failing you—abandoning you—the moment we arrive.'

'I'd have understood.'

'I know, but…' He raked a hand through his hair, wanting desperately to change the subject. 'What do you think of your quarters?' She had a sitting room, a bedroom and a lavish bathroom, all decorated in mother-of-pearl and lapis lazuli. 'Do you approve of them?'

She glanced around, her hands twisting together. 'They're very beautiful—rooms fit for a princess.'

If she married him, she would be a princess.

As if realising that, some of the colour leached from her face. Was it the thought of marrying him that caused it, or the thought of becoming a princess?

And, if it were the latter, why would that frighten her? He'd had women tell him that becoming a princess was a dream, a fantasy akin to winning the lottery.

'There are things here I don't understand…undercurrents with your parents.'

'I… Yes. I thought that in four years things might've changed, but…' But it was as if no time at all had passed. And he felt damned to hell because even now, at any moment, he expected Ahmed to sweep into the room and pull him into a bear hug.

Sarah strode across to an arched window. Her room had a view onto a beautiful courtyard, but when she turned back to face Majed he realised she'd not even seen it. He could see her wishing herself a million miles from him and Keddah Jaleel.

In three strides he was in front of her and gripping her shoulders. 'Trust me, Sarah, please. I don't have time to explain it all to you now. We're expected soon in my father's private sitting room. What I can say is that I didn't go with my mother because I wished to present a united front with you first. I don't want them to doubt where my loyalty lies. I want to tell them our news and then I'll humour my mother with as many private interviews as she wants. I promise.'

She pulled in a breath and finally smiled, but he saw what it cost her. 'Please tell me I have time to shower and change?'

'Only just. I'll be back to collect you in twenty minutes.'

She nodded. 'You're right. We should get this over with as soon as possible.'

He reached out to trace a finger down her cheek. The memory of their almost-kiss on the plane flared back to life between them. He dragged his hand back from temptation. 'You're not facing a judge, jury and executioner, *habibi*.'

She rolled her eyes, but he suspected it was more an effort to ignore—and deny—the heat flaring between them than anything else. 'No, it's just your parents. And they're *way* scarier.'

And yet, somehow, she could still make him laugh.

'So you are pregnant, then? It's as we feared, Rasheed.'

Majed's heart pounded when his mother strode to the window, her back ramrod-straight. He'd expected his father to be the one to pace, the one whose voice would be strained with disapproval.

Before Majed could speak, Sarah said, 'Your Highness—'

'We do not stand on ceremony in here, Sarah,' Rasheed said. 'In private you must call me Rasheed and my wife Aisha.'

Sarah blinked. 'That's very kind of you. I—'

'And you must allow me to offer you my felicitations.'

To Majed's surprise his father rose, took Sarah's hand to bring her to her feet and embraced her. If he hadn't seen it with his own eyes, he wouldn't have believed it.

'Congratulations, Majed.'

Majed shook the hand his father offered him, feeling as if he'd stepped into a dream.

'Do the two of you plan to marry?'

Sarah glanced at him and it was only the steadiness reflected in her eyes that unglued his tongue from the roof of his mouth. He read her intent to step into the breach if needed, but he had no intention of appearing weak or feeble in front of either her or his father. 'We've not decided yet.'

His father sat with a heavy sigh. 'It will be a great scandal if you do not.' His glance towards Sarah, however, was not unkind.

'Nonsense.' Aisha spun around. 'These things can be hushed up.'

Rasheed continued as if Aisha hadn't spoken. 'I know things are done differently in your country, Sarah, but it will be a scandal whichever path you choose.'

His mother's eyes flashed and Majed readied himself to intervene as she came storming back towards them, her eyes fixed on Sarah. 'You will steal my son from me!'

'Mother!'

'No, Majed, don't.' Sarah swallowed and nodded, but not in agreement with his mother. 'That's what my mother accused Majed of too, though she phrased it differently. And it's not my intention to steal your son from you, Aisha. I've come to your country to see…to see if there's a place for me here. To see if I could live here.'

His mother stilled for a moment. With a smooth, graceful motion she sat and folded her hands in her lap, although her chest rose and fell furiously. 'You would consider moving to Keddah Jaleel rather than forcing my son to turn his back on his birthright?'

Rasheed shot to his feet and started to pace.

And, though he cast a dark glare at her, Aisha stoically ignored him.

Sarah nodded. 'It's why I'm here.' She turned to Rasheed, who still paced, a frown darkening his face. 'I want you to know that your son has acted honourably. He's asked me to marry him. It's I who have yet to come to a decision.'

Majed moved to stand beside Sarah. 'I'll not have Sarah pressured. She'll have the freedom to make up her own mind without interference.'

Sarah stared at him with those big blue eyes as if he were a super-hero. It made him stand taller.

His mother waved an imperious hand. 'Oh, do please sit down, Majed. You're looming and it makes my neck ache.'

He saw Sarah seated first and then sat beside her. All the while he was aware of his father's dark gaze.

Aisha cleared her throat. 'Sarah will be free to make up her mind. As free as the rest of us are.'

He stiffened. 'She's not bound by our laws.'

'No, but you are, my son. And Sarah needs to be aware of the repercussions to you of her decision. It's only fair that she knows all the facts before she makes a decision.'

Sarah stared at Majed and then Aisha. 'What repercussions?'

Majed took her hand—a show of solidarity—but his heart pounded and his nerves stretched tight. 'I'm interested to hear those myself.'

She squeezed his hand and it helped to steady the nerves jangling through him.

His mother shot him a sharp look. 'You know them as well as I do. If you do not marry the woman who bears your child, our people will see it as a sign of weakness and moral degradation. Your father has fought for reform in this country and he needs an heir who is strong—who is seen by the people to be strong. There are those still wedded to the old ways who would use any perceived sign of weakness as a reason to incite civil unrest.'

His heart pounded. At least his mother saw a role for him in the governance of his country. *If he married Sarah.*

Sarah's white-knuckled grip on his hand tore at him and, while he appreciated the truth of his mother's words, he wished she'd held her tongue. 'You need to decide what will be best for you, Sarah—for you and the baby—not for me. And there is time yet before that decision needs to be made. Don't forget that.'

Her grip eased and she nodded. Her low, 'Thank you,' pierced him. He admired her courage in the face of his parents' stateliness, and her veneer of steadiness in the face of her own panic.

'But it *will* need to be made. And *soon*.'

'Mâmâ!'

'And…and if I do decide to marry Majed…?'

His heart clenched with a fierceness that took him off guard—part possessive triumph and part primal, masculine desire that she would be in his bed, that he would have the right to make love with her every single night.

He rubbed his nape and tried to get his rampaging hormones back under control. He was no better than his marauding forebears!

'If I marry Majed will your people see him as a strong ruler—will they see him as someone who can take their country into the future? Will they follow him?'

'It's impossible, my dear.' Rasheed moved back to his seat. 'Our people will never accept a Western woman as their Sheikha.'

Each of his words pounded into Majed like

blows. The fact they weren't true made no difference.

'They would come round if *you* showed your support!' his mother all but shouted in Arabic. 'She could show our women a new way, a way forward.'

In Arabic, his father told her to hold her tongue. Majed had never heard him speak to her in such a hard tone before.

Majed squared his shoulders. 'So you still do not see a place for me here? You refuse to countenance me as your heir?'

'I—'

'Stop!' Sarah surged forward to stare into the older man's face. 'What are you doing?' she whispered, and this time it was Majed who felt he didn't understand the undercurrents in the room.'

'You are welcome here, Sarah, but you are an outsider.'

'She's not an outsider.' Majed shot to his feet. 'She's bearing your grandchild.'

His father's chin lifted and his eyes flashed. 'And as such she is entitled to my care, my consideration and my assistance. She also has my gratitude. But it is the same now as it was four years ago, Majed. I plan to make your cousin, Samir, my heir. You are free to return to the West.'

Sarah stared at Rasheed in growing horror. What was he doing?

And why was he doing it?

From the stricken expressions on Aisha and Majed's faces, not only had he hurt them—'gutted' would be a more precise description for them—but he was going against some kind of traditional royal protocol.

'You cannot!' Aisha had gone deathly pale. 'The ruling sheikh hasn't done that in over two hundred years, Rasheed!'

'Hush, Aisha, it's for the best.'

How could this possibly be for the best?

Thank you for bringing my son home.

No!

Sarah clapped her hands, turning all eyes to her. She made herself smile—not over-brightly, because she couldn't manage that, but enough to cover her confusion. 'Majed, your mother has long desired a private interview with you. She hasn't had the opportunity for four long years. Surely it's time to grant her wish now that we've announced our news?'

Majed opened his mouth but she cut him off.

'I'll be perfectly fine. I'm not a child that needs looking after. Besides, I'm very much looking forward to getting to know your father better.'

Rasheed's head came up. 'As much as I echo that sentiment, I'm afraid it will not be possible this afternoon. I have state business that demands my attention.'

A likely excuse if she'd ever heard one! 'You don't have ten minutes to spare for the mother of your future grandchild, sir?'

She hoped he'd correctly interpret the almost-glare she sent him. If he didn't give her ten minutes of his time now, she'd speak her mind in front of everyone...and she had a feeling he'd hate that.

But she refused to hold her tongue. She and Majed might not love each other—and they might not marry—but he was her friend and she was on his side.

'How delightful,' Rasheed murmured. 'I'm sure I could spare you ten minutes, my dear.'

They were said pleasantly enough, but Sarah had a feeling his words were forced out through gritted teeth.

Majed and Aisha left, and Rasheed led her into an even more splendid room than the one they'd just left. But if he thought the pomp and splendour would intimidate her then he was sadly mistaken. 'What on earth are you doing?' She rounded on him. 'You've lost one son. Why on earth would you want to banish another?'

He paled at her words but drew himself up to his full height and stature. 'You know nothing of the politics of my country or my family.'

'Oh, no you don't, Rasheed.' She was too het up to stand still. She paced up and down in front of him and stopped to point a finger at him. 'You might be supreme ruler of Keddah Jaleel, but at the moment you're simply Majed's father. I care about Majed and I care what happens to our baby.'

His gaze lowered to where her hand curved about her abdomen and before her eyes he seemed to age. Her heart thumped. Biting back something rude, she took his arm and led him to a sofa embroidered in such rich cloth it almost distracted her from her aim of talking sense into Rasheed.

'I know you love your son, so why would you banish him from the homeland he loves?'

The older man stiffened. 'I do not banish him.'

'That's exactly what you're doing if you deny

his right to ascend to the throne when the time comes.'

Rasheed stare back at her stonily.

Had nothing she'd said made any impact on him? She gripped her hands together. 'Would it really be so problematic if the heir took a Western bride?'

His gaze slid away.

'If the answer to that question is yes...' She swallowed. 'Then the solution is simple. I'll leave Keddah Jaleel and never return. I'll deny Majed all access to his child.'

Rasheed surged to his feet. 'You cannot do that. It would kill my son.'

The way he'd said 'my son' gave her hope.

'And, as Aisha said, it can all be hushed up. No one need ever know that Majed has a child. If we take that course of action, it should surely remove what you see as a major stumbling block to Majed succeeding you.'

The Sheikh's chest rose and fell. 'You cannot deny him his child!'

She didn't know what she was searching for... 'Though, I suppose, Majed and I could continue to live here in Keddah Jaleel. I'm certain Majed could find a role here, even if it wasn't as the supreme ruler.'

Rasheed's face tightened and he slashed a hand through the air. 'That is out of the question!'

Behind the anger she sensed something else but she wasn't sure what. Fear? Resentment? Regret? Her mouth dried. 'Do you really think Majed would make such a poor ruler?' Did he not know his son at all?

Rasheed's chin shot up and for a moment she swore she saw affront in his face, before it became opaque and calm once again—his statesman's face, she suspected. He lifted his arms. 'What do you want of me, Sarah Collins?'

What did she want? She pushed her shoulders back and refused to dwell on the fact that she was berating a supreme ruler and interfering in the politics of a country she didn't understand. 'I want you to give Majed a chance.'

'A chance to do what?'

She moistened parched lips. 'A chance to prove that he should be your heir.'

'And if I do not do this?'

'Then I'll leave. And I'll make sure I never see Majed again.'

Her heart thumped. What on earth was she

doing? What if the Sheikh told her to go now and pack her bags?

She pressed a hand to her stomach and glanced about the stately room. 'I refuse to be responsible for denying Majed his birthright.'

'Instead you will deprive him of his child!'

'It is you, sir, who tells us this situation is impossible.'

He rose to stalk about the room. Something in the slant and set of his shoulders reminded her of Majed so much that an ache pressed against the backs of her eyes.

Rasheed swung around but his stately reserve crumbled when he stared at her. 'My dear, do not cry.'

She lifted her hands to her cheeks, surprised to find them wet. A lump stretched her throat as she tried to mop them up. 'I'm sorry.' To her mortification the words emerged on a sob. 'Pregnancy hormones—they're making me all…all emotional.'

He sat down beside her and patted her hand. 'Do not distress yourself. It cannot be good for you or the baby.'

'Oh, Rasheed, don't you want to know your grandchild?'

'Of course I—'

He broke off and folded his arms, his brow lowering. 'You are either very clever or very ingenuous.'

She dried her eyes. 'I suspect I can be both at different times, but I'm not trying to trick you into admitting anything you don't want to. I'm just wanting to do what is best for my baby. And the best for Majed. And myself too.'

'In that order?'

She smiled. 'Now I think it's you who's trying to be clever. The baby comes first. As for the rest…' She lifted her shoulders and let them fall.

For a moment, silence stretched between them. Sarah's heart thumped and her temples ached. On impulse she reached out and touched Rasheed's arm. 'I'm sorry Ahmed is no longer with you. I wish he were. I know how much Majed wishes it too.'

Rasheed went grey but he didn't pull his arm away. She must be breaking a hundred royal protocols but she didn't care. 'I can't imagine the pain of losing a child.'

'I pray you never will.'

She met his gaze. 'Please don't punish Majed because he isn't Ahmed.'

A wall came down in those eyes and Sarah couldn't help feeling she was missing something significant, some piece of the puzzle that would give her the clue she needed to understand. Before she could try and work it out, Rasheed had risen and was offering her his arm. She took it and followed him as he led them back the way they'd come.

Aisha and Majed broke off when she and Rasheed entered what Sarah guessed must be Aisha's private sitting room. One glance at Rasheed's face and they rose. If possible, their faces grew even more serious.

'Zawj?'

Husband. It was one of the few Arabic words Sarah knew.

Beside her she could feel the tension radiating from Rasheed. 'Majed, Sarah has convinced me to reconsider my position.'

Aisha clapped her hands beneath her chin, her eyes glowing.

'She has convinced me to give you a chance.'

'A chance, sir?'

'You have the next month to prove that you're willing and able to step into my shoes, to prove you should be the heir to the throne of Keddah

Jaleel—to prove that you can rule with courage and love.'

Relief ripped through Sarah. Majed's expression, though, turned opaque.

He gave his father a short bow. 'I will not let you down, Bábá.'

Had Majed and Aisha heard the Sheikh's sigh? Something in it tugged at Sarah's heart.

'Sarah.' The Sheikh turned to her. 'If my son does prove himself worthy, you need to know this...'

'Yes, sir?'

Her heart started to thump. Would he banish her and the baby?

'To ascend the throne, Majed must marry you.'

Her heart leapt into her throat to pound there, making it impossible to speak.

'This is not blackmail. It is the tradition of our people. It is the only way Majed will be able to maintain the respect and loyalty of his subjects. Do you understand?'

She couldn't speak but she managed to nod.

'If you'll excuse me now...'

The Sheikh left and Majed immediately moved to her side, his eyes scanning her face. 'You're pale. And you're shaking. Come, sit down.'

He pressed a glass of cold water into her hand and she sipped it gratefully.

'Are you feeling better?'

Dark eyes peered into hers but she could read nothing in them. It was as if Majed had closed himself off from her. Why didn't he look happy or relieved, or something positive?

'Would you like to see a doctor?'

'Don't fuss, Majed. I'm fine. It's just… I've never… Well, your father…'

'The situation has been nerve-racking, yes?' Aisha supplied.

The warmth in her smile settled Sarah's nerves more than anything else could have done. 'Exactly. But I think perhaps the worst is over now.'

Aisha reached out and patted Sarah's hand. 'I think so too. Majed, you should take Sarah back to her room to rest for a bit. I'm looking forward to getting to know you better, Sarah.'

Majed didn't speak on the long walk back to Sarah's quarters. Not once. He didn't speak until he'd seen her seated in her sitting room. 'What did you say to my father?'

She lifted a shoulder and let it drop, trying to smile. 'Probably things that in the olden days would've had me beheaded.'

His lips lifted, as if by rote, but the smile didn't reach his eyes. Her stomach started to shrink.

'We've not had capital punishment in Keddah Jaleel for more than a century.'

'That's a…um…comfort.'

He didn't even attempt to smile this time. His eyes blazed into hers. 'Sarah?'

His tone was even but relentless. It told her he meant to get an answer to his earlier question, and he meant to get it soon.

She bit back a sigh. 'I told him that if he didn't give you a chance to prove yourself that I'd… um…'

He folded his arms. 'That you'd…?'

She swallowed, her throat suddenly dry. 'That I'd leave Keddah Jaleel and…and deny you all access to the baby.'

The lines about his mouth turned an ominous shade of white. 'I see.'

She suppressed a shiver as his eyes froze over.

'Did you mean that?'

'I don't know.'

'So you *lied* to him?' The light in his eyes was utterly relentless. 'Either that or you've lied to me.'

'I was just trying to make things…better.'

'*Better?*' He stared at her as if she spoke a language he didn't understand.

She lifted her chin. *In for a penny...* 'And I told him it wasn't fair to punish you for not being Ahmed.'

His mouth dropped open. 'You. Did. *What?*'

He flung his arms outwards, each word shooting from him with bullet-like precision, piercing her with his incredulity and censure. He paced the room, letting forth a torrent of Arabic that she didn't understand but which sounded far from complimentary, and her shoulders started edging up.

He swung back. 'You've no idea what you've done, do you?'

Evidently not.

'You've all but promised to marry me if he makes me his heir. You've all but promised him and my mother that you'll raise our child here in Keddah Jaleel. And if you don't keep your word now you'll break their hearts all over again. Not only have they lost a son, but now they must lose a grandchild?'

'No, I—'

'You told him I want to be his heir and you've promised him I'll fulfil the role!'

He paced the room, muttering imprecations under his breath. She tried to claw her panic back under control. All she'd done was defend him, stick up for him. What was so bad about that?

He turned, his eyes black. 'You've made all of these promises on our behalf and neither one of us yet knows if we can keep them, let alone live up to them!'

Her mouth dried. 'You don't want to be the ruling sheikh?'

His hands slammed to his hips. 'Do you know yet if you want to marry me?'

No.

'Precisely,' he shot back at her, as if he'd read that thought on her face.

She'd thought she was making things better. Instead she'd made them worse. *Flake. Disappointment. Failure.* The words pounded at her, making her feel small and stupid.

He slashed a hand through the air. 'You've no idea in what you're meddling. You shouldn't have interfered!'

That put steel back into her spine. 'Then why don't you tell me? Why don't you fill in the blanks I'm so obviously missing? In Australia you told me you were your father's heir, and then

I get here and find out there's a whole big question mark over the issue. If you don't give me all the information, Majed, how on earth do you expect me to negotiate the situation here?'

He didn't want her negotiating the situation! He'd negotiate it for both of them.

Even as he thought it, though, he knew he wasn't being fair.

Sarah hadn't meant to put him in a difficult position. All she'd done was fight for the chance she thought he wanted. She'd stuck up for him, had shown loyalty...and he was railing at her like a martinet.

'It's all well and good for you to reprimand and slam me, but I at least told you what to expect from my mother.' Her eyes flashed. 'I didn't throw you in at the deep end without any warning!'

Yes...but she'd told Rasheed to stop punishing him for not being Ahmed. He wanted to drop his head to his hands and howl.

Her chin shot up. 'You don't trust me, do you? Despite all your promises of friendship and whatnot, you don't trust me enough to tell me what's going on here.'

She moved in closer, her eyes continuing to

flash. Her scent bombarded him and he had to grit his teeth against it.

'How on earth do you think we're going to successfully co-parent if you keep important information from me?'

His heart pounded so hard his chest started to hurt.

She folded her arms, her glare increasing. 'Why does your father have such an issue with you becoming the next sheikh? And don't even think of putting me off, Majed. Whether you like it or not, this is going to affect our baby. You *will* tell me the truth.'

Or what? She'd leave?

He bent at the waist, hands braced against his knees to draw deep, ragged breaths into his lungs.

When he glanced up, he found she'd pressed a hand to her brow as if to keep a headache at bay. She was pregnant. She needed to rest—for her own sake and for the baby's too.

She won't rest until you tell her every loathsome, repugnant detail.

He straightened. 'I hate talking about this.' The words left him on a growl but that didn't seem to perturb her in the least.

'That much is evident.'

He motioned for her to take her seat again. 'To understand my father's attitude, you need to become better acquainted with the circumstances surrounding Ahmed's death.'

CHAPTER SEVEN

SARAH'S KNUCKLES TURNED WHITE. 'I know this can't be easy to talk about.'

Yet she still meant to make him utter the words out loud. Majed swung away. 'I told you it was a woman who was responsible for leading Ahmed to the rebels.'

'Yes.'

He stared at a spot on the wall and forced himself to continue. 'I was the one who introduced Fatima to the palace…and to Ahmed.'

Her gasp—loud in the silence of the room—speared into him.

'My father blames me for that. As he should.'

'No, Majed, you're wrong. Even a stranger can see—'

'Let me finish!' The words left him on a bellow, but he couldn't help it. 'There's more to this sordid story yet.' *So much more.* 'I was the one dating Fatima.' His lips twisted and he finally turned to face her, steeling himself for the condemnation and pity he expected to see. 'I was the one who fancied himself in love with her.'

Her jaw slackened. 'She betrayed you with Ahmed?'

Yes. Which meant Ahmed had betrayed him too.

His skin felt as if it were on fire. He tried to bury the pain coursing through his chest, pounding at his temples, threatening the strength of his knees. 'Obviously the rebels' sights were initially set on me, but when Fatima found she had access to a greater prize—the Sheikh's actual heir—she took her chance.'

She stared at him and it was almost impossible not to shift under that gaze. It made him tense... and the tension made him cruel. 'Have I satisfied your curiosity?'

Her head reared back. 'Curiosity? Is that what you think this is?' She shot to her feet. 'I can't believe you let me go in front of your parents without telling me this. I'd never have said the things I said to your father if I'd known.' She dragged her hands through her hair. 'How insensitive and... and *cruel* he must think me.'

She broke off to pace. His heart thumped. She was right—it hadn't been fair. But talking about

Ahmed and Fatima tore the very heart out of his chest and…he couldn't bear it.

His heart pounded. Sarah had stood up for him. She'd had the courage to defend him. A strange warmth filtered into his veins, warming him from the inside out. Majed loved his father but he knew how intimidating Rasheed could be. Sarah had promised him friendship and she'd delivered. While he…he dragged a hand through his hair…he'd put her in an impossible situation.

He pinched the bridge of his nose. 'I'm sorry.'

She swung back. 'Because you're afraid I'm going to leave?'

His hands fell back to his sides. 'Because I promised you friendship and I fell at the first hurdle.'

She stilled.

He moved across and took her hands. 'You deserved better from me. You deserved my full disclosure. I've been weak. Talking about Ahmed is…it's very painful for me. I've avoided talking about this for the last four years. I can see now how wrong that was. I'm sorry my weakness put you in such a difficult position.'

Her hands trembled. 'Wow, you can do a really good line in guilt when you want to.'

She said it to make him smile and he did his best to oblige her. 'I'm an expert.'

He said that to make her smile, and something in his chest started to ache when she managed a weak one.

'I want you to know I'm grateful for the opportunity to work with my father.' He squeezed her hands lightly and then released her, stepping away before he pulled her into his arms and tried to erase the events of the day in the mind-boggling pleasure of making love with her. It might work in the short term, but in the long term it would probably prove a disaster. He had no intention of doing anything that might make her leave. He did his best to banish the images from his mind. 'You'll stay?'

She stared at him for a long moment, before nodding. 'For the moment.'

His knees almost gave out in relief and gratitude. 'Thank you.' *Do not kiss her!* 'I should leave you now. You should get some rest.'

'Sarah?'

Majed tapped on the open door to Sarah's sitting room. She glanced up from her seat on the sofa where she was flicking through a magazine.

She closed the magazine and sent him a guarded smile that had his chest cramping. She gestured him into the room. 'Good morning.'

'Did you sleep well?'

She started to nod and then slumped back. 'About as well as you did, I expect.'

'Things will get easier. I promise.'

She nodded.

'Which makes what I'm about to say all the harder.'

She tossed the magazine to the coffee table. 'You better give it to me straight. I've been banished or—'

'Nothing of the sort. My mother can't wait to show you about the palace and introduce you to the women of the family.'

'But your father?'

'I haven't spoken to him since our interview yesterday.' He grimaced. 'However, ten minutes ago one of his aides informed me that I'm to take up the mantle of my royal duties today.'

She straightened. 'Oh, wow. But…that's good, isn't it?'

He didn't know. He hoped so.

'But you're feeling bad because you believe you're abandoning me?'

Bingo.

'Don't worry about me, Majed. I'll be fine.' She suddenly smiled. 'I expect your mother will make sure of that.'

So did he. It was just… *He'd* wanted to be the one to introduce her to his country.

'I can tell them it's impossible for me to take up my duties until next week.'

'You'll do nothing of the sort!' She shot to her feet. 'It's obvious this is a test.'

'Of my—?'

'Of *our* determination and…and steadfastness.'

She made it sound as if his father was trying to scare them away. She could have a point.

'Do you have time to talk?'

He'd make time. 'Yes.' He sat.

She sat too. 'I've been going over things.'

He didn't want her going over things. He didn't want her worrying and stressing. He wanted her… He bit back a sigh. He wanted her to fall in love with Aisha and his country, and to leave all the hard stuff to him.

But Sarah wasn't built like that. So he'd simply have to find a way to ease her mind about whatever was worrying her.

'I want to have a *difficult* talk.'

He lifted his chin. He had no intention of shying away from a difficult discussion again. He set his shoulders. 'Shoot.'

She pulled in a deep breath. 'You think your father holds you responsible for Ahmed's death.' She moistened her lips. 'You think…you think he can't forgive you.'

She was spot on, but his throat had closed over and he couldn't speak. He nodded.

'I think you're wrong.'

The certainty in her voice had him glancing up. He fought the urge to yell and fling wild words at her. She didn't deserve his anger. She deserved his gratitude. If it weren't for her, they'd be back on a plane bound for Australia, and who knew when he might've stepped foot on home soil again?

She moved to stand in front of him and he realised he'd shot to his feet. He stood there with hands clenched at his sides, breathing heavily. His feeling of vulnerability appalled him but he could not do anything about it. Talking about the events of four years ago had ripped the scab off a wound that would never heal and it made him want to tear at rock with his bare hands.

She reached up and touched his cheek, laid her

hand flat against it, and her warmth seeped into him, helping to ease the storm raging in his soul.

'You've suffered so much. You all have. My family is fractured but that's because my parents have allowed their bitterness to consume them. It means I can recognise that kind of vitriol. There's something different happening with your family, Majed. I'm not sure what it is, but between us maybe we can work it out.'

And then she removed her hand and retreated back to the sofa, staring at him expectantly. Swallowing, he nodded and took the seat beside her. 'I'm listening.'

Her gaze never wavered. 'This is going to take courage from you.'

He stiffened. 'I am no coward.'

'*Emotional* courage.'

His jaw clenched. Was that her opinion of him? 'As I said, I'm not a coward.'

'But your feelings have been hurt. You believe your father blames you for Ahmed's death because you blame yourself. That's colouring your judgement.' She lifted a hand skyward. 'You think I've just called you a coward when I don't believe that for a moment.'

His head rocked back. His mouth dried. 'I wasn't aware I took offence so easily. My apologies.'

'I don't want your apologies, Majed. I want you self-aware and concentrating. Something is happening here and we need to get to the bottom of it.' She dragged in a breath. 'My child's happiness depends on it.'

'*Our* child,' he corrected.

She stilled and then nodded. 'Our child.'

'Go on.'

Those steady eyes of hers speared him again. 'You need to put your sense of guilt and blame to one side for the moment—discount them if at all possible. Can you do that?'

He couldn't explain why, but her calm logic helped to ease the storm raging within him even further until it was nothing more than a distant rumble on the horizon. 'I can try.'

Her smile anchored him.

She turned to him more fully. 'The first words your father spoke to me were, "thank you for bringing my son home".'

His jaw dropped. His heart started to thud.

'And then, to you, he acted all cool and regal and distant.'

He recalled her bafflement at the meeting and it started to make sense.

'Why would he hide his joy, his happiness, at seeing you *from* you? It makes no sense.'

If what she said was true…

'Of course, you were just as cool and regal and distant in return.'

His mouth dried. Should he have given his father more? He suddenly saw what she meant by emotional courage. Did he have the courage to allow himself to be completely vulnerable to his father…and risk rejection? Again.

'I told your father that if it were truly impossible for you to rule with a Western wife I'd return to Australia without you, deny you access to the baby, and we could all keep the baby's paternity secret.'

His hands clenched so hard his entire frame shook. 'Did you mean that?' *She'd deny him his child?*

'Keep your mind focussed on your father for a moment.' Her voice had gone sharp. 'He was utterly horrified that I would even consider doing such a thing.'

His breath got caught midway between his chest and throat.

'He told me I couldn't do it. He said denying you your child would kill you.'

He had?

'If you had to choose between your kingdom or your child, Majed, which would you choose?'

'My child.' He said it without hesitation.

'And your father knows that.'

Hence the reason for his reprieve.

'Because I'm pregnant, my mind is filled with thoughts of our child. My love for it…all I'd endure and suffer for it if I had to. So when I look at your father and find his words and actions in relation to you in such conflict, I ask myself, what's causing it? I ask myself, what does he fear?'

Majed's first thought was that his father feared his second son wasn't up to the task of leading his country. But that was the old guilt—the doubts Sarah had asked him to put to one side.

'What kind of father was he when you were growing up?'

'Loving.' He half-smiled at the memory. 'He was strict too, but he was also loving. He made time for his family, despite the many demands of his position. He said his family was his strength.' Ahmed's death had struck him and revealed his most vulnerable site—it had devastated him.

Majed tried to breathe through the pain raking his chest. 'It's possible he's still grieving. Perhaps he's not yet ready to move on. Nobody can replace Ahmed. The idea is ludicrous but...'

'But someone will need to step up and be ruler when your father's reign comes to an end,' she finished for him.

Was it possible that Rasheed didn't blame Majed for Ahmed's death? Could it simply be that his younger son's presence reminded him so forcefully of his older son's absence? It was a possibility Majed hadn't considered. His heart pounded so hard he found it difficult to breathe. 'I have to make this right. I'm not sure how, but my father deserves peace.'

She nodded and it hit him then that if it weren't for her he'd have never had this insight into his father. He'd have continued to wallow in a sea of self-pity. Sarah had forced him to look beyond his own hurt and instead of despair he'd discovered hope. He gripped her shoulders. 'I cannot thank you enough. I hadn't thought of looking at it in a different way.'

'You don't need to thank me. I'm simply trying to make things as good as they can be for our baby.'

His mind was no longer on the baby but on her. It occurred to him now that he wanted to marry her for *her*, not just because of the baby. He wanted her in his bed every night. She might not be a native of Keddah Jaleel but she'd make him a fine wife.

As if aware of the direction of his thoughts, she scrambled out of his grip and across to the sideboard to pour herself a glass of water. He followed. He didn't mean to, but something stronger than rational thought made him move across to her. Without giving himself time to think, he swept the swathe of hair from her neck to press a kiss there.

Her gasp arrowed straight to his groin.

The glass clattered to the counter and both her hands clutched the sideboard, as if for support.

He grazed his teeth lightly across her earlobe, breathing her in deeply.

'What…what are you doing?'

Her chest rose and fell. She wanted him just as much as he wanted her. He couldn't explain the craving in his blood where she was concerned but it helped that she felt it too. 'I am kissing you, *habibi*.'

'But…why?'

She stiffened, so he ran his hands from her shoulders down to her hips, pulling her back against him so she could feel the hard length of him against her back, glorying when she arched into the kisses he pressed to her neck. 'I want you, Sarah. I want you like I've never wanted any woman before.'

A moan broke from her lips. 'You said you wanted all or nothing.'

And she couldn't promise him that yet...

They both stilled. For a moment the next move hung in the balance. He could make love to her now, as his aching flesh longed to, with no promises made. Or...

With a groan, he stepped away from her and the action felt like a physical pain. 'I'm sorry. Forgive me. I forgot myself.' Regardless of what his barbarian forebears might've done, he couldn't seduce Sarah into marriage. She needed to make that decision with her head, not her hormones.

She was going to be the mother of his child.

She'd won him a major concession from his father.

She didn't deserve pressure or coercion. She deserved his support.

He glanced at his watch. 'It's time for me to

go. An aide will be along in half an hour to take you to my mother. I wish you an enjoyable day.'

With that, he turned on his heel and strode from the room.

One week later Majed strode along the corridor leading to the women's quarters. He had aunts and cousins who lived here and others who often came to visit. He hoped they'd taken Sarah to their bosoms, praising their life in Keddah Jaleel and making her want to live here too.

He'd not spent anywhere near enough time with her this week. He'd wanted to introduce her to the delights of his country but instead he'd found himself swamped with royal duties—meeting overseas delegates, taking part in trade negotiations, overseeing the introduction of a science, technology, engineering and maths syllabus at a new women's university in the capital.

He'd relished every moment of it. But it didn't change the fact he hadn't spent enough time with Sarah.

Maybe she was relieved with the current state of affairs. Maybe she was as afraid as he was that they'd give into the overpowering temptation of their desire for each other…afraid of the consequences that might bring.

His mother had kept him abreast of Sarah's activities—most of which she'd taken upon herself to arrange. Earlier in the week they'd visited a master artisan at his textile shop. Majed's lips lifted. Sarah had waxed lyrical about all she'd seen. The artisan had sent her back to the palace with bolt upon bolt of material. She'd been overwhelmed at the generosity. Little did she realise the prestige that came with the title Royal Supplier.

His mother and several of her aides had taken Sarah on a tour of the undercover markets. She'd returned smelling of incense and he couldn't help wishing he'd been able to share the experience with her—to witness her delight and curiosity. Rather than talk about her own experiences, though, she wanted to hear about his.

Did she recognise his new sense of purpose? Did she sense that he'd found the place where he belonged? For the last four years he'd felt cut adrift from all that mattered. Now he felt as if he were finally fulfilling his destiny. And that was all down to her.

Without a single doubt in his mind, he knew

now he wanted to be his father's heir. He wanted to lead his country into the future and see his father's—and Ahmed's—vision for Keddah Jaleel become a reality.

He'd stayed away for so long in an attempt to bury the pain of his father's perceived rejection and in the process he'd buried his true desire—that he wanted to take over the throne from his father when the time came. This was his destiny.

Did she sense all that? Did it frighten her?

If so, she gave nothing away. What she wanted to know was if he and his father had *talked* yet.

So far, Majed had to answer in the negative. He'd spent a great deal of his time in his father's company, but never alone. Twice he'd requested a private interview but both times he'd been stonewalled. He'd ask again soon. Eventually Rasheed would grow used to his presence. And then, maybe, they could work on rebuilding their personal relationship.

Music drifted from the large common room at the end of the corridor. It wasn't traditional Keddah Jaleely music. It wasn't even Arabic music. It was… He frowned. And then he laughed. It was kitsch Western pop music.

He moved to the doorway and his grin widened at what he saw. Half a dozen women—his mother included—were following Sarah's lead in a series of dance moves that had them all laughing and breathless.

The pop music was completely out of place in this room with its richly coloured decorative tiles, arched windows and carved columns, yet the women had such large smiles and the music was so much fun that he had no words for the sense of wellbeing that flooded him. Sarah was...

Dear God! He gulped. She was wearing a traditional Bedouin dancing girl's costume in pale blue with a silver-and-lapis-lazuli medallion belt riding low on her hips. The costume left her belly bare and drew the eye to her generous curves.

Desire fireballed in his abdomen. He backed up a step. He shouldn't intrude...

'Majed!'

His mother's greeting prevented his retreat.

The other women in the room all spun to him with smiles of welcome. Sarah sent him a half-grin—as if to share the joke of a disco in an Arabic palace with him—but a moment later her cheeks flamed pink and she attempted to cover her bust, and all that delicious cleavage, with her folded arms... Then she seemed to realise that her stomach was bare and her hands flew down to cover it.

She stood there staring at him with eyes too big for her face, one foot rubbing the top of her other in delicious awkwardness, and a wave of tenderness washed over him. Her pregnancy hadn't started to show yet, but he'd done research on the Internet and he knew that she'd develop a baby bump within the next couple of weeks.

He couldn't wait to feel the baby kick. He hoped she'd let him share that with her.

'Majed,' his mother murmured in an undertone. 'It's impolite to stare.'

He started to find that Sarah's cheeks had gone even redder. The other women didn't know why Sarah was here, but there'd be speculation. They knew Sarah was his friend.

And now he'd added fuel to the fire.

Sarah cleared her throat. 'We've been having a cultural exchange. Your cousins have been teaching me how to belly dance.'

He noticed then that Sarah wasn't the only one wearing a traditional dancing girl's costume.

'While I've…' Her grin peeped out again.

'While you've been polluting their ears and minds with *pop music*.'

She shook her hair back, feigning superiority. 'I'll have you know that this isn't just any pop group, thank you very much. They're *the* pop group.'

As she spoke, she strode over to a nearby chair and pulled on a shirt that buttoned down the front, hiding all her delicious curves from sight. Majed wanted to go down on his knees and beg her not to.

Sarah's pulse fluttered in her throat like a crazy, wild thing. The hungry twist to Majed's lips, the way he surveyed her as she buttoned her shirt— the gleam in his eyes—made her want to incite him to action—make him haul her into his arms and kiss her. And not stop.

Dangerous.

The word whispered through her.

But delicious.

Very.

But she had her baby's welfare to consider and muddying the few rational thought processes she could muster with hormones… Well, it would be irresponsible. And she was trying so very hard to leave that part of herself behind.

She pulled in a breath. She needed to create a

better family for her baby than she'd had. She would not give her child a legacy of warring parents and bitterness—a sense of always being pulled in two different directions. They all deserved better than that.

Friendship first.

She pasted on a smile. 'We've been having a lot of fun today. Your family's hospitality is boundless. An offhand comment about needing to buy a pair of wireless speakers, or a wistful remark that my sewing machine is in Australia, and—*voilà!*—these items seem to magically appear!'

He blinked and a sigh welled through her. He had such beautiful eyes.

'Sewing machine? You've taken up your old hobby again?'

'Oh!' She shook herself. 'Just a…whim.' She waved what she desperately hoped was a nonchalant hand through the air. His eyes narrowed and she rushed on. 'After coming home with all that gorgeous cloth the other day, I…'

'Come and see what this remarkable girl can seemingly whip up out of thin air.'

Aisha took Majed's arm and led him towards the other end of the room where two sewing machines and an over-locker had been set up for

Sarah's benefit. Her pulse went into hyper-drive. 'Oh, I'm sure Majed isn't the least interested in my silly little bits and bobs.'

He glanced at her, one devastating eyebrow cocked. 'Then you'd be wrong.'

'Bits and bobs!' Aisha scoffed. 'Majed, the girl is an absolute marvel. She could be an artisan herself.'

Ha! Sarah's heart crunched up tight. She gave what she hoped was a light laugh. 'A flattering exaggeration.' But it was still an exaggeration.

Aisha's brow furrowed. She said something low to Majed that Sarah didn't catch but it had his gaze turning thoughtful.

'Look at this.' Aisha held up the piece Sarah had spent the morning working on. 'Is it not stunning?'

Majed took the creation, his hand travelling thoughtfully over the material, and Sarah had to force her attention away from his hands...and the thought of how they'd feel if they moved over her naked flesh with the same appreciation. A shiver shook through her.

'Granted, it's pretty.' She shifted her weight from one foot to the other. 'But that's really down to the material. It's flawless. And a delight to work with.'

He turned to her. 'This is…it's remarkable! Why must you put it down?'

She snapped her mouth shut, her heart pounding.

'I'd no idea you could do such fine work. What inspired this piece?'

It was a riff on a kaftan. Many of the women in the palace wore gaily coloured kaftans. But this one had a Western influence. 'I was just playing with the idea of East meets West.'

She had to swallow. She did all she could to tamp down the old enthusiasm that rose through her. Nothing could come of it. It would only lead to disappointment. She had a baby on the way, for heaven's sake! She'd given up such folly long ago.

'And?'

She shrugged. 'I love the style of dress here—the long kaftan shirts and the loose, flowing trousers, the long, sheer scarves. They look so comfortable, but I love Western styles as well. I wanted to create something I could wear that was…' She searched for the word.

'A compromise?'

'A complement—the best of both worlds.'

'We want her to make us all one.'

She gestured to the piles of fabric nearby. 'I'd be delighted to. All you need to do is choose the material you'd like.'

Sarah reached out and took the tunic from Majed. 'It's not really finished yet. I've not finished off the seams properly and…and other things.' She showed him a seam to prove her point. 'But we've just been playing and experimenting and having some fun in the process.'

He opened his mouth but she hurried on. 'How has your morning been? I'll warrant ours has been more enjoyable.'

'The kaftan is not the only thing Sarah has made this morning.'

To Sarah's discomfit, Aisha handed Majed a tiny baby's nightie made from the softest cotton threaded with a yellow silk ribbon at the bodice. 'The detail is breath-taking,' Aisha continued. 'Just look at these pintucks.'

She doubted Majed knew what a pintuck was. In fact she doubted Majed even heard his mother. She couldn't speak as she stared up into his stunned and suddenly vulnerable face. She knew he was imagining their child in that nightie. He was imagining holding their baby, seeing it for the first time…and the hunger in his eyes hollowed out her heart.

He loved this child as much as she did.

How could she deny him the chance to co-parent, to be a part of his child's everyday life?

Could a marriage based on friendship be enough?

And desire. Friendship *and* desire.

But desire didn't last…

She snapped back when Aisha said her name, to find everyone surveying her. 'I'm…I'm sorry. I was a million miles away.'

Aisha smiled but Sarah wasn't sure why. 'Would a cruise down the River Bay'al be to your liking this evening? The worst of the day's heat will be gone and it's cool on the river. And very pretty. We're rather proud of it.'

How could she say no to that? 'I'd love to. It sounds wonderful.'

A gleam briefly lit Majed's eyes. 'I'll collect you at six,' he said, before turning on his heel and disappearing.

'It sounds delightful.' She turned back to Aisha with a determined smile. 'What shall we wear?'

'Not we, my dear—*you*.'

It would be just her and Majed? A traitorous

pulse leapt at the thought. Wouldn't it be dangerous, the two of them alone together...?

She folded her arms. Majed, her *and* all his staff. They wouldn't be alone. She did her best to quash her disappointment.

'I think you should wear this.' Aisha took the tunic from Sarah's limp fingers. 'And I think you should make those trousers you were describing to us.'

Another riff on the ones the women here wore—except a little more fitted and cropped just above the ankle.

'We're eager to see them. We're eager to see what they'll look like on. Please, my dear, put us out of our suspense.'

'By all means.' Everyone had been so kind that it was the least she could do. And she had a feeling that keeping busy for the rest of the day would be a very good idea. When she sewed the rest of the world fell away, and she found she needed the comfort of that today.

She turned to the piles of fabric. 'We have so much to choose from and—'

'But only this will do.'

Aisha pulled forth a black silk, so finely made it was almost sheer. Sarah could imagine how decadent it would feel against her skin—like a lover's caress. She could imagine Majed's eyes darkening in appreciation when he saw her in them. It would set off the myriad blues in the tunic perfectly. Without a word, she took the fabric, spread it out and set to work.

'I need to pinch myself.' Sarah kept her voice low, not wanting to disturb the twilight hush of the river. To the west the sky was a burst of orange, slowly shading to breath-taking pinks and paler mauves. All the colours were reflected in a river that was millpond-smooth. Something about it eased the burning in Sarah's soul.

'You like it?'

Majed's caramel voice bathed her skin in a warmth that lifted all the fine hairs on her arms. 'Like it?' She started to laugh. What wasn't there to like? They were drifting down the river on a slow-moving barge reclining on a bed of silken cushions beneath a canopy of blue-and-silver satin. The luxury was unimaginable and the scenery stunning. '*Like* is far too weak a word. I...' She swallowed. 'I can't believe how beautiful it is.'

Date palms, tall, majestic and seemingly ancient, lined the riverbanks. Beyond them stretched a fertile flood plain green with crops. Majed had told her the river was a hub of activity during the day, with trading boats that travelled from the south, but at the moment it was quiet with only an occasional pleasure craft or tradesman's boat to share its great breadth with them. The palace security patrol ensured that nobody could approach the barge.

'It is beautiful.' Majed turned to her, surveyed her from beneath lazy brows. 'You're beautiful too, *habibi*. I'm honoured to share this with you.'

Majed wore traditional robes and a headdress, and her heart had nearly stopped when she'd first clapped eyes on him. He looked like a stranger— a beautiful, exotic stranger. His robes highlighted the masculine breadth of his shoulders and the lean, hawk-like angles of his face.

A great thirst welled up inside her. 'Um...thank you.'

He rested back against the cushions on one elbow and turned more fully to her. A pulse started up in her abdomen. With a deliberate finger, he reached out and traced a path from her knee to her mid-thigh. She sucked in a breath. 'What are you doing?'

The smile he sent her could only be described as wolfish. 'I like to touch you…and the clothes you wear invite me to touch them. Was that not your intention?'

'Of course not.' Her pulse hammered. *Liar.* 'Don't be ridiculous.'

'That's a shame.'

He held out a dish of delicacies to her—locally made Turkish delight that melted on the tongue, dates that were fatter and more luscious than any she'd ever had and a pastry, whose name she couldn't pronounce, which was filled with nuts and honey and tasted of the gods. Normally she'd have eaten her fill, but not this evening. Majed unsettled her too much. 'No, thank you.'

He selected a pastry and bit into it slowly, his tongue snaking out to collect a stray flake from his lips, his gaze on hers the entire time. He made a murmur of appreciation that was so lover-like, heat flooded her cheeks. She swallowed convulsively. 'What are you doing?' she whispered. She wanted to look away, but she couldn't.

He finished the pastry slowly, deliberately… and with obvious relish. 'I promised myself that I wouldn't pressure you one way or the other into marriage with me, Sarah, but I think that was a mistake.'

'Oh, I don't! I think—'

His finger against her lips halted her words. 'I think you ought to know how invested I am in you marrying me. I think you ought to know how much I want you in my bed.'

She jerked away from him, her heart thumping hard. 'Stop it.'

'Why? Because when I talk to you like this you find it hard to hold onto your own restraint? Find it impossible to ignore your body's demands?' He smiled, as if he'd read the affirmative answer in her face. 'Good. I burn for you, *habibi*, and I want you burning for me too.'

He leaned towards her, dredging her with the scent of amber and spice. 'If I were an old-time sheikh I'd order the sides of this canopy lowered until we were cocooned in our own private world and I'd have my wicked way with you until you were replete with pleasure.'

The picture he created was so vivid in her mind, her lips parted to draw in more air.

He leaned back. 'You're lucky I'm a more civilised man than my forebears.'

Was she?

Of course she was!

Her heart thumped. It took a moment for her to master her voice. 'You forget we have a baby to consider.'

His nostrils flared. 'I do not forget that for a moment. Our child is always on my mind.'

Of course it was. He wanted the baby, not her. She couldn't forget that.

Oh, no, he wants you too.

In his bed but not in his heart. Could she settle for that? She cleared her throat. 'Be that as it may, we need to decide what will be best for this baby.'

'And why do you doubt that marrying me won't be in our baby's best interests? If you marry me our baby will have a privileged life. He or she will want for nothing. Every opportunity will be open to him or her. What could be better than that?'

His eyes flashed and an answering frustration pierced her. 'Parents who love each other,' she shot back.

He rolled into a sitting position. 'That is impossible. Besides, your parents must've loved each other once and looked what happened to them. We can give our child a more solid foundation. We can give it parents who respect each other.'

Respect? She bit back a sigh. Respect was *important* in a relationship. So why did it sound so…dreary?

'We can give this child a family, Sarah. Brothers and sisters.'

She'd wanted a tribe of siblings when she was growing up. She could have all the things she'd wanted from a family *now*…if she put aside girlish daydreams and fantasies.

It didn't seem too much to ask, did it?

CHAPTER EIGHT

'I WILL DO everything in my power to make you happy, Sarah. I mean that.'

The expression in his eyes told her he meant his words. He was no longer trying to convince her through the force of their desire for each another. He was no longer trying to cloud her judgement by leaning in too close and making her blood leap and her pulse pound.

It should've made her happy! Majed was vowing to do everything in his power to ensure that she and their child would have not just a good life but a wonderful life.

Except give you his love.

She swallowed. Why did that have to matter so much? Love would come. It would evolve naturally from mutual respect and friendship.

Oh, but it would be a pale imitation of what she'd expected whenever she'd thought about love and marriage in the past.

But…

Maybe Majed was right. Their relationship would never descend into the bitter acrimony that her parents' marriage had. Hadn't she vowed to do anything to spare her child that?

'Tell me more about this old design ambition of yours.'

She glanced across at him. He half-reclined against the cushions and stared out at the river as the barge slid across the water. He looked lazy, at ease…almost slumberous. It occurred to her that she'd not seen him the slightest bit relaxed since they'd arrived in Keddah Jaleel. It soothed something inside her.

She crossed her legs and reached for a piece of Turkish delight. 'Oh, it was just a phase—like wanting to be a firefighter when I was ten or a mermaid when I was seven.'

'You wanted to be a mermaid?'

His slow grin warmed her blood…and her heart. Pressing both hands to her chest in exaggerated longing, she said, 'Desperately,' making him laugh. And then she popped the Turkish delight into her mouth before it melted in her fingers.

He leaned forward to pour her a glass of exquisite home-made lemonade. 'How old were you when you decided you wanted to be a designer?'

'Fourteen, I think.' It was hard to feign nonchalance but she did her best. 'I always loved making things—as a kid I loved anything crafty.' The desire to make pretty things had always lived inside her, but it wasn't until she'd discovered sewing that it had really flared into life, filling her with a sense of purpose. 'I intended to study design at university.'

'You didn't?'

'I started.' She sipped her lemonade, hoping its sweetness would help counter the bitterness of the disappointment that could still rise up inside her all these years later, reminding her what a flake she was...what a failure.

Her heart thumped and she risked a quick glance at Majed's profile. He deserved a better wife than she'd ever make—a more polished and accomplished wife.

'You started?'

His gaze speared hers, belying the laziness of his posture, and for a moment it felt as if he were plumbing the depths of her soul and laying bare all her secrets. She dragged her gaze from his, feigning interest in a passing cargo boat.

She forced herself to continue. 'I completed a year of study.' And, according to her marks and her teachers, she'd been doing well... 'But in the summer break my mother organised for me to be an intern with Inguri Ishinato.'

He refilled her glass. 'The famous designer?'

She nodded and made herself smile. 'She's wonderful, isn't she?'

'I don't know. Some of her creations seem outrageous for outrageousness' sake. But I understand that she has an enviable reputation.'

'Oh, she was a name all right. Working at her studio opened my eyes.'

'You didn't enjoy your experience there?'

Quite the contrary. She'd loved it but...

'You decided it wasn't the right career for you?'

She rolled her eyes in an attempt to mock herself, doing her very best to smile with wry self-awareness. 'If we hadn't sworn to be honest with each other, I'd be tempted to lie now and save my battered ego, but the truth is I don't have the talent to be a designer. At the end of the internship Inguri took me aside and told me I was a very competent seamstress, but that my design talent was mediocre at best.'

Majed shot into a sitting position. 'She what?'

'She suggested I'd find it more rewarding to make dress-making a hobby rather than a career, and more profitable to find work in a different field.'

He stared at her. 'So you quit design school?'

His disbelief made her fidget. 'It seemed the wisest course of action.'

'Wise?'

He stared at her with such unmitigated astonishment her shoulders started to hunch.

'One setback! You let one person's opinion dissuade you from pursuing your dream?'

She'd bet once Majed set his sights on something he wouldn't let anything or anyone dissuade him. But she wasn't like him. 'It wasn't just any person, Majed. It was a world-class designer whose opinion I valued.' Inguri Ishinato had been her hero.

He folded his arms, his nostrils flaring in the twilight. Her heart lurched. The man was magnificent, truly magnificent. But she wished he wouldn't stare at her like that.

'My mother had been warning me for years that the industry was cutthroat and fickle...and how difficult it would be to earn a decent living. So I decided to be sensible.'

'And learn office administration instead?'

His lip curled and he spat out the words as if they tasted bad on his tongue. She shoved her shoulders back. 'It's a skill that's always in demand. The qualification I got ensures I'll always be able to find work. You can scoff at that all you like, Majed, but it's something I refuse to take for granted.'

'But does it fill your soul? Does it chase the emptiness away?'

She flinched and threw up an arm as if to ward off his words. How could he use her confession against her like this? It was...cruel!

He reached out, his fingers shackling her wrist. 'Is it really that easy to deter you from striving towards what you want? Do you really lack the confidence—the courage—to try?'

He stared at her...almost in fury...and her mouth dried.

'If I started a campaign to undermine your confidence in your ability to be a good mother, would you give way so easily?'

'Don't be ridiculous!' She shook off his hand. 'That's completely different.' She *loved* this baby.

You loved designing too.

His face turned cold and pitiless. 'Your mother

didn't appear to approve of your career choice. Did you never question her hand in helping you to acquire this internship with Inguri Ishinato?'

His meaning was clear and her stomach clenched. 'My mother would never sabotage me like that.'

'She didn't need to sabotage you. She simply put a single roadblock in your path. And you crumbled with barely a whimper.'

He was wrong about that. It was just that she'd kept her whimpers to herself.

'I haven't seen a sewing machine in your apartment. I've never even heard you speak about designing or sewing until recently.'

'My equipment was packed away in my move. I haven't got round to unpacking it.'

The fact of the matter was that she hadn't had the heart to look at her sewing machine after Inguri's pronouncement. She'd put her things away and had let the emptiness grow. She'd resisted the temptation to dabble—how could she just dabble when it meant so much more to her than that? She'd not been able to face it until here, now, in Keddah Jaleel, where her old world had dropped away. With all of that delicious fabric tempting her...calling to her. Today when she'd sewn, she'd felt at peace—and whole—for the first time in years.

There had been one other time.

The pulse fluttered in her throat. When she'd made love with Majed, the empty places inside her had filled then too.

But that had to have been an illusion.

'You have a fear of failure.'

The disgust in his voice snapped her spine straight. 'Everyone is afraid of failure, Majed, even you.'

'It won't stop me from trying, from striving, from doing my very best and giving my all.'

Her heart started to thump. Did he think her incapable of those things?

Well...aren't you?

She didn't give her all in her work—it was so darn boring and unchallenging that she found it hard to remain engaged—but her employers deserved better than that. The realisation made her reach out a hand to steady herself against the cushions.

She didn't give her all in her relationships either. She was always waiting for someone to find fault with her. If they didn't, she saved them the time by pointing out her myriad flaws first—all under an umbrella of humour and self-deprecation, of course. But it created a distance inside her that was impossible to breach.

She swallowed. Was that what she wanted to teach her child?

At nineteen she'd let someone deter her from following her dream and she hadn't felt whole since. And yet, not once had she dared to resurrect her dream.

Because she lacked courage.

When had she settled for being a flake and nothing more than a flake?

'I want to be the best father I can be to our child. I want to be the very best role model I can be.'

The iron in his voice pounded at her.

'I also want to be happy. I want to show my children that they can be happy too. You, Sarah—I think you're afraid of being happy.'

Pain radiated out from her chest to all her extremities—even the tips of her fingers and the soles of her feet ached. 'I'd like to return to the palace now.'

Her words emerged clipped and short... distant. Without even looking at her, Majed gave the order to return to the palace. They didn't speak a single word to each other again until they reached the palace and Majed gave her a clipped, 'Goodnight.'

Her throat had closed over so she couldn't return the pleasantry. Not that it mattered. He strode off so fast, he'd not have heard it anyway.

Sarah returned to her rooms to find one of Rasheed's aides waiting for her. 'Sheikh Rasheed understands from the Sheikha that you have a desire to become acquainted with the palace protocols and duties surrounding the role of the Sheikha?'

'Um…' She stared at the file the man held out to her. It was so thick!

'He had this compiled for your benefit.'

She took it, her heart sinking. 'Please thank His Highness for me. It was very considerate of him.'

The aide bowed and left.

Sarah carried the file to the desk and stared at it. Majed's reproof rang in her ears before she'd even lifted the cover.

As she read, her heart sank further and further.

Sarah didn't clap eyes on Majed for the next two days. Her lips twisted as she sewed the seam for a

sleeve. No doubt he was trying to find a way tactfully to retract his offer of marriage. The thought
made her heart burn though she didn't know why.
It would make things simpler all round if he did.

The plan had been for her to shadow Aisha
these past two days but, for reasons she wasn't
privy to, those plans had been cancelled. At
Majed's command, perhaps? But nor had Aisha
gone about her duties, leaving Sarah to the mercy
either of her solitude or the other women's min-
istrations. Instead, she declared herself on holiday and spent her time in the women's quarters
with Sarah and whoever else felt like joining
them. They all urged Sarah to work at her sewing machine, to show them the things that she
could make, to teach them some of the techniques they admired.

She complied gladly, though Majed's reproof
about being afraid to be happy constantly rang
in her ears. Sewing—making clothes, handbags,
cushion covers and other soft furnishings—*did*
make her happy. Why had she denied herself this
pleasure so completely? Why had she turned her
back on it?

'May I have a word, Sarah?'

Majed's voice sounded next to her and she

jumped, nearly sewing her finger to the tunic she was making for Aisha.

'Forgive me, I didn't mean to startle you.'

He didn't look angry, for which she gave thanks. Instead he looked... Actually, she couldn't decipher his expression. But she could guess the contents of the conversation they were about to have and she couldn't prevent her heart from sinking.

This is for the best.

Of course it was, but...

She stood. 'Of course.'

She expected him to lead her to a quiet corner of the room but he led her out to a private courtyard instead. A fountain tinkled in the quiet air and the cool shade beckoned a welcome invitation. She gave a low laugh. 'You've chosen a pleasant spot for your unpalatable news, Majed.' She appreciated that, appreciated his thoughtfulness in providing her with this shield of privacy.

'I don't know what you mean. What *news* do you think I have come to give you?'

He'd accused her of a lot of things—being afraid of failure, of not fighting hard enough for what she wanted—all true. But she refused to be a coward now. She turned to face him. 'After our discussion on the river the other evening, I expect you've come to retract your marriage proposal.'

He paused in the act of motioning her to a bench padded with brightly coloured cushions. 'You are most wrong, *habibi*.'

The whispered promise of the endearment softened her stomach. She wanted to sit, to move away from his overpowering masculinity and the need it sent rocketing through her, but he took her hand and she found she couldn't move a muscle.

'Would that news have been unpalatable to you?'

Oh, um... Before she could concoct a reply, he lifted her hand and pressed a kiss to her wrist at the point where her pulse jumped and jerked. He grazed it with his teeth and she could barely contain a gasp.

'I'm fully committed to marrying you, Sarah Collins. The final decision rests with you. If you choose to not marry me, it will hurt me very much.'

She reclaimed her hand. It would hurt his pride, not his heart.

Though, that wasn't completely true. It would hurt him if she denied him his child. Not that she'd ever do that, but... It would hurt him as

MICHELLE DOUGLAS

191

much as it would hurt her, and that knowledge plagued her.

'No, *habibi*, I came to apologise.'

Apologise!

'For the things I said two evenings ago. It was wrong of me. It shames me to remember them. I've no right to judge you. I've had privileges you could only have ever dreamed about. I've had parents who encouraged me to strive for whatever it was I wanted. The disparity in our backgrounds...' He shook his head. 'I had no right to call you a coward.'

He sat and, resting his elbows on his knees, he dropped his head to his hands and muttered what she suspected was some kind of curse in his native tongue.

She sat too and touched his arm. Warmth immediately sparked through her fingers and she reefed her hand back. 'There was truth in your accusations, Majed. I didn't want to admit it then, but—'

'No!'

He spun to look at her and slowly he straightened. Something in his eyes made her mouth dry.

'You're no coward. You lack confidence, that's all. And it's *that* which made me so angry. Not at you,' he rushed to reassure her, 'but at the circumstances in your life that have robbed you of believing you've the right to chase your dreams, that have prevented you from recognising and taking pride in your own talents.'

The regret in his face touched her.

'I'm sorry I railed at you like I did. I—'

'Stop, Majed. Stop feeling so bad about this. I accept your apology. I also accept that there was truth in some of your words—even if I didn't like hearing them.'

He took her hand. 'But the failings aren't your fault. You've not had anyone to believe in you and encourage you...until now.'

Something in his tone... She straightened. 'What do you mean *until now*?'

'I've invited the master artisan you visited the other day to view the things you've been making for my mother and the other women. He's with them now.'

Sarah shot to her feet, her heart pounding. 'You've done what?'

She'd only just rediscovered her love for all of this. She wasn't sure she could bear anyone putting a dampener on her joy just yet and telling her she had only a mediocre talent. Which made no sense at all, because she hadn't had any delusions of grandeur while she'd been playing with all of that gorgeous fabric. And that was what it had felt like—playing. There'd been joy, freedom and fun, nothing more.

'You're angry with me?'

You promised honesty.

She swallowed. 'Hiding behind anger would be easier than facing the truth.'

She went to stride away—to pace up and down the courtyard—but he caught hold of her hand and, before she knew what he meant to do, she found herself tumbled onto his lap. Warm arms encircled her. Warm lips hovered just centimetres from hers...so tantalising and tempting. The scent of amber and spice surrounded her.

'I enjoy having you in my arms, *habibi*, and I could very easily lose myself in you this very minute.' The words growled out of him. 'But that would be unforgivable.'

She'd forgive him!

He stroked the length of her jaw with one lazy finger. Beneath it her blood heated. 'You're afraid the artisan will damn your work with faint praise.'

She nodded, not trusting herself to speak.

He stared down at her solemnly. 'I don't know what he'll say. He's promised to provide an honest assessment, that's all.'

Her heart jerked in her chest.

'But I want you to know that, whatever he says, my opinion of you won't change.'

She stilled.

'I'll still admire you, regardless of his assessment of your skill. I'll still enjoy your company and the way you make me laugh. I'll still think you intelligent, warm and generous.'

Very carefully—as she was sitting in his lap and they needed to be careful when they were this close to each other—she shuffled into a more upright position. It brought their mouths closer together. His gaze rested on her lips for a moment. He swallowed and she saw the effort it cost him to control himself. A ripple of triumph quivered through her.

His lips curved. He said something she didn't understand then. 'If you agree to marry me, I'll look forward with much pleasure to our wedding night.'

'You'd make me wait that long?'

'It is the custom of our people. I must honour you with every token of reverence and esteem.

But there can be pleasure to be found in delayed gratification.'

He leaned forward and grazed his teeth across her ear. Heat shot straight to her core and need pounded through her with a prickling awareness that made her want to press against him to assuage the ache, to inflame him, to incite him to lose control. If she did that… The fat file Rasheed had sent to her rose in her mind. Biting back a sigh, she pressed a hand to Majed's chest and pushed him back. Beneath her palm his heart raced just as hard as hers.

He glanced into her face and murmured something under his breath. 'This is a dangerous game we are playing. Come.' He gently lifted her to her feet. 'Let us go and see what our artisan has to say.'

Us. Our. The sense that they were somehow in this together lent strength to her knees. She pushed her shoulders back and ignored the craven urge to flee. She'd face this with the same courage that Majed faced the future.

The moment they entered the common room, an elderly man raced over to them, his face alight. 'Your Highness Sheikh Majed, who is this talent you have found? What is his name? I would take him for my apprentice in a heartbeat if he is free to engage in such study.'

'Arras, that is a great honour.' Aisha moved to stand beside him, sending Sarah a speaking glance. 'You have to understand that Arras has not taken on an apprentice in more than five years.'

The older man shook his head. 'I am getting old and I'm not as patient as I once was. I give my time now only to the extraordinary. And, while some of this work is raw and undeveloped, it has a great energy and sophistication that mark it as an exciting talent.'

Sarah couldn't believe her ears. She'd forgotten to pull her hand from Majed's upon entering the room, and she gripped it now as if her life depended on it. She didn't care what rumours it would excite among the women.

Arras glanced at their linked hands and he broke out into a radiant smile. 'It is this lovely young lady who possesses this talent, yes?'

'It is.'

The pride in Majed's voice as he introduced them made everything inside her feel bright, as if she had her own internal sun. 'You...you really like my pieces, Arras? You think they have promise?'

'I do, yes! Come, come.' He hustled her over to the table that held the pieces Aisha had evidently assembled for him. 'I'm impressed with the East-West fusion of this tunic…'

They spoke for nearly two hours, the rest of the world receding as they discussed design principles and techniques. Before he left, Arras pressed his card into her hand. She promised they'd talk again soon.

When he was gone, it was only she and Majed left in the common room. He sat on a deeply cushioned sofa but he rose when her gaze founds his.

She pressed a hand to her chest. 'You did this for me?'

She didn't know what to say. She was absurdly close to tears. How could she thank him for all he'd done? He'd helped her to overcome her worst fear. And in facing it she'd discovered that her most cherished wish could come true. That it was true—she had a unique and remarkable gift—and she no longer intended to deny it. In that moment the emptiness that had been a constant part of her since she'd given up on her dream vanished. She'd found what she was destined to do.

Could she do that *and* be Majed's Sheikha?

'I told you I'd do whatever I could to make you happy. I meant that.'

'Wouldn't your people have a problem with the Sheikh's wife doing…that?' She waved a hand towards her sewing machine. 'With her having a career beyond her royal duties?'

'I see no reason why they should.'

She stared at him and her heart started to pound, thumping relentlessly against the walls of her chest. Wind roared in her ears, blocking out everything but the truth. She loved Majed. She loved him heart and soul. She loved *his* heart and soul. She loved his kindness, his sense of honour and his unselfishness. She loved his confidence and his ability to solve problems, his ability to meet obstacles with his head held high. She loved his…big-heartedness.

A vice tightened about her chest. But he didn't love her.

Does it matter?

She swallowed. Of course it mattered. But it didn't mean she couldn't marry him.

Rasheed's fat file rose in her mind, and a sigh pressed against her throat, but she refused to let it escape.

'Sarah?'

She shook herself. What on earth was she doing just standing here like a dummy? She made herself smile and then she strode across to him. Placing her hands on his shoulders, she reached up to press a kiss to his cheek. His eyes glittered, his lips parted and for a moment she thought he'd sweep her into his arms and kiss her senseless. She stepped back quickly, the blood thundering in her ears. 'I…' She had to swallow. 'Nobody has ever done such a thing for me before. I can't tell you how much it means to me.' She shrugged, unable to find the words. 'You're an amazing man. I feel lucky and blessed to know you.'

'I feel exactly the same way about you.'

Not *exactly*. And that stung in ways she hadn't known possible. But she did have his friendship and his respect. And there was little doubt that he desired her.

He reached out, as if to touch her cheek, but his hand fell short and dropped back to his side. She knew why. The spark between them was too strong. A single touch could unleash a raging inferno. But there was too much at stake. She couldn't get this wrong. This wasn't something she could screw up.

Her hand curved about her abdomen, unconsciously protective. For once in her life she had to be as unlike a flake as possible. Majed's eyes lowered to where her hand rested. When he lifted them they glowed with a possessive pride.

'You make me believe impossible things are possible,' she blurted out.

He nodded. 'Good.'

'I…I need to go somewhere quiet and process all of this.' She turned and made for the door.

'Sarah.'

She pulled in a breath before turning to face him again.

'There is time. You have time. I don't want you feeling pressured. I don't want you feeling stressed.'

Even now, when he must sense how close her capitulation was, he thought first of her welfare.

He didn't love her, but maybe she had enough love for both of them.

She had to work out what she wanted. And then, somehow, she had to find the courage to fight for it. With a nod, she left.

Majed stood in front of his father. For the last three weeks he'd worked tirelessly at his father's side. The older man hadn't given him a single word of praise, but he had sought Majed's opinion on several tricky issues. Majed didn't flatter himself that it was because his father valued his opinion. It was all part of a larger test. He just didn't know yet if he'd passed or not.

He squared his shoulders. He'd given it his all. He'd made no secret of the fact he wanted a role in taking Keddah Jaleel into the future. He'd held nothing back.

'Greetings, Samir.'

Majed's gut clenched as his cousin—older than Majed by two years—entered the stateroom. Everyone else had been ordered to leave, even the Sheikh's most trusted aides.

The cousins clapped each other on the shoulder in greeting. Majed loved and trusted his cousin.

'As you both know,' Rasheed started, 'I intend to choose one of you to be my heir.'

'Sir—' Samir started, but Rasheed held his hand up for silence.

'As you must be aware, I have long favoured you, Samir. You're smart and steady, and loyal to the people of this country. You'd lead our people well.'

'Thank you, but—'

Again that hand rose, demanding silence.

Majed glanced at his cousin's profile. Samir didn't want the title—not at what he considered to be Majed's expense. Last week the two of them had engaged in a long and serious discussion on the topic.

'Majed, in these past weeks you've proven yourself adept and surprisingly canny in foreign affairs.' Rasheed's lips momentarily pressed into a thin line. 'Additionally, Samir has informed me that if he does become ruler of Keddah Jaleel he envisages a role for you among his trusted advisors.'

It was the role he'd have played if Ahmed had lived. It was what he'd been trained and groomed for. There was no hiding the displeasure in his father's eyes, however, at that prospect.

Majed wanted to throw his head back and howl. Did his father still hold him so comprehensively responsible for Ahmed's death? Would he never forgive him? Did the sight of his younger son still cause him so much pain?

To spare his father, maybe he should leave Keddah Jaleel for good. *Which would kill your mother.*

It was all he could do to stop his shoulders from sagging.

In the next moment he pushed them back. What of his child's destiny? Did his child not have the right to know and love this land as much as Majed did? He'd fight any battle for his child's welfare and honour.

Rasheed blew out a breath, his dark eyes troubled. 'Majed, if Sarah agrees to marry you, then the throne will one day be yours.'

A fierce gladness gripped him. His father had seen his worth! Majed would work tirelessly to prove to his father that his faith had not been misplaced. 'Thank you, Bábá.'

'I believe you're as committed to bringing democracy to this country as both I and Ahmed.'

Pain raked his heart at the mention of his brother but he forced his chin up. 'I am. I'd infinitely prefer that Ahmed were here, but he's not.' He broke off, fighting the burning in his throat. 'Thank you for giving me the opportunity to prove myself.'

At Majed's mention of Ahmed, Rasheed lowered himself to the seat behind his desk, his hand covering his eyes. When he lifted it away, Majed was shocked to see how old his father looked. He wasn't old! He was only sixty-three!

'Majed, if Sarah decides not to marry you, I'd ask that you leave Keddah Jaleel.'

Ice tripped down Majed's spine, vertebra by vertebra.

'I'll not make it an order, but there will be a scandal that our enemies will do their best to use against us. I cannot let that happen. I'll not allow your brother's death to be in vain.'

CHAPTER NINE

'THIS IS AMAZING!'

Majed glanced across at Sarah as she peered out of the helicopter's windows, straining against her seatbelt in her efforts to take in the view, and was glad he'd taken the time away from his duties to show her more of the land he loved.

They'd been in Keddah Jaleel for three weeks and two days now. He needed to know if Sarah had come to a decision. He needed to know if she was going to marry him.

Don't pressure her. You've no right to pressure her.

His grip tightened about the helicopter's control stick. It was one of the most difficult things he'd ever done—maintaining this façade of patience and calm, of not doing all he could to sway her decision...or to not sway it more than he already had.

But if she left Keddah Jaleel with his child...

His stomach lurched. He couldn't bear the thought.

He knew she wouldn't keep their child from him. There'd be visits and holidays, but he wanted to be a part of their child's everyday life—an integral part, not a figure on the edges.

He swallowed. He'd shown her the beauty and luxury of life at the palace—the lifestyle she could enjoy as his wife. He'd tried to show her the kind of consideration and respect she would receive from him as her husband. He'd demonstrated that she could pursue her dreams and carve out a career for herself here too.

He hadn't pointed out how much more difficult it would be for her if she decided not to marry him, if she returned to Australia instead. His heart clenched at the thought. She already knew those difficulties—had lived through them with her own mother. Even if they shared custody, life would still be far more difficult.

For them both.

He'd avoided mentioning how much her decision would affect his own destiny.

That'd be emotional blackmail.

He hadn't mentioned the scandal that'd break once it was known that the Sheikh's only son had a child out of wedlock. He hadn't told her of the press storm that would explode, the fact it would follow her to Australia…or that an intense media interest—and presence—would follow their child throughout his or her life.

He refused to terrorise her with such horror stories. At the moment her health had to be his primary concern. She should be entitled to make her decision in peace.

'This is such a contrast to Demal.' She breathed.

Her awe reached him through the headsets they wore. He manoeuvred the helicopter lower so she could observe the landscape at closer quarters.

'This is what I imagined Keddah Jaleel would look like.'

They'd left behind the capital with its fertile coastal plain, green fields and glinting river to pass over the high hills to the west. Here the topography changed dramatically to an arid rocky landscape that eventually merged with seemingly endless dunes of shifting, golden sand. A heat haze shimmered in the distance.

He glanced at her again. 'What do you think of it?'

'It's utterly terrifying. Like Australia's Great

Sandy Desert. I can't imagine how awful it would be to find yourself stranded alone in it.'

He opened his mouth to tell her she need never fear such a thing when she swung to him.

'It's utterly magnificent. It's so...*beautiful*.'

She saw the same beauty in this landscape as he did and something inside him shifted. He feigned preoccupation with the myriad dials on the helicopter's control panel, but his heart started to pound. This woman had an uncanny ability to get beneath his skin.

He'd dismissed it as desire. Well...he hadn't exactly *dismissed* it.

He wanted her. His desire for her burned through him, hot and fierce. It kept him awake at night. He hadn't *dismissed* that desire but he'd used it to explain away his other reactions to her—other more disturbing reactions.

He clenched his jaw. She was carrying his child. It was only natural he should feel possessive and protective but he couldn't allow that to compromise his common sense, his caution or his ability to reason—the way those things had been compromised with Fatima. The way Ahmed's ability to make good decisions had been overset by his brother's girlfriend.

That Ahmed had betrayed Majed demonstrated the evil that accompanied such a passion. It showed the selfishness and the potential for self-destruction that resided at the heart of such passion. He ground his back molars together. He wanted no part of that kind of love again. He'd dig out every grain he found forming within and he'd destroy it.

If Sarah married him, he'd become Keddah Jaleel's ruling Sheikh. Sarah's welfare, their children's welfare and his people's welfare would rest with him. It would be his duty to protect them and keep them safe. They deserved the very best he could give them. They deserved his very best efforts. He would not fail them.

'Majed?'

Sarah stared at him with pursed lips, a question in her eyes. She'd been speaking but he hadn't been attending to her words. He swallowed. He wouldn't allow himself to fall in love with her, but nor would he neglect her.

Visions of exactly how he wouldn't neglect her rose in his mind. Heat and perspiration prickled his nape. He needed a long, cold drink. 'I'm sorry, *habibi*. It's been a long time since I flew a helicopter. It's requiring more concentration than I remembered.'

The purse of her lips became more pronounced—*those luscious lips!*—and an ache stretched through him, pulling his nerves taut. A teasing light deepened the blue of her eyes. The fact she was oblivious to his preoccupation should've comforted him but it only strained his muscles further.

'Exactly how long has it been since you flew a light aircraft? Should I be worried?'

He laughed—how could she make him do that? 'I think we can risk it. There's the oasis now. See how it emerges from the desert like a jewel?'

An hour later they were sitting beneath a fringed canopy that protected them from the fierce heat of the sun. A small breeze made the fringe dance and cooled their hot flesh as it made its way across the deep pool of water in front of them. They sat on silken cushions scattered across a brightly coloured carpet that Sarah had spent an inordinate amount of time studying. That was, until she'd suddenly spun to him and started pelting him with questions. How many people lived at this oasis? How many people did it service?

How did the people here make a living? How many oases like this one were scattered across the Keddah Jaleely desert?

He'd answered each of her questions as best as he could until he found the opportunity to ask one of his own. 'From where does all of this interest spring?'

She glanced out at the water before taking her time to select a date, but something in her face had become shuttered. He leaned towards her. 'Sarah?'

Her shoulders suddenly drooped. 'I feel so utterly ignorant about everything, Majed—Keddah Jaleel's people, your country's history, its geography…and everything! There's so much to learn.'

He started to laugh. 'You don't need to learn it all at once. You don't need to learn it at all if you don't want to.'

She rose and he found himself staring at a very rigid back. Glancing around, he dismissed the attendants. They melted away without a sound. Rising, he moved behind her. Placing his hands on her shoulders, he pulled her back against him.

For a moment he thought she might resist, but then she softened and nestled back, and he had to grit his teeth at the desire that fired through him. 'Would you like to tell me what's troubling you?'

He felt rather than heard her sigh. 'Not really.'

Instead of pressing her, he simply pulled her more firmly against him, one of his arms encircling her just below her collarbone, and he just held her, running his other hand from her shoulder to her elbow and back again in an attempt to give her comfort…and a safe haven in which to relax. They stood like that for a long time, staring out at the sparkling sheet of water. Very slowly, the tension drained from her. A fierce gladness gripped him. He always wanted her to find comfort in his arms.

Eventually he said, 'In another five days we'll have been in Keddah Jaleel a month.'

She nodded and her hair tickled his face. 'The time has whizzed by so quickly. More quickly than I thought it would.'

Did she mean she wasn't yet ready to make a decision?

'But I know in five days' time you'll ask me again if I'll marry you.'

There was something in her voice. He turned

her to face him. 'Do you doubt my desire to marry you?'

She searched his eyes and then shook her head. 'No.'

He couldn't help it. He traced his right hand from her shoulder and up the clean length of her throat to cup her jaw. Her pulse quickened beneath his fingers and his own leapt in response. 'Do you doubt our ability to deal well with each other?'

She shook her head again and the warm slide of her skin against his fingers pulled something tight inside him.

'No, I don't doubt that. The fact is…'

The sudden vulnerability in her eyes caught at him, though he sensed she tried to shield it from his sight. 'The fact is?'

Her lips lifted as if they couldn't help it. 'The fact is I…I like you.'

Both of his hands cupped her face as he wrestled with the sudden fierce joy that gripped him. 'You like me?'

'I know it doesn't sound like much, but—'

'It is everything!' And then he couldn't help himself. He kissed her. He'd meant it to be nothing more than a swift press of his lips to hers, but her surprised gasp sent warmth washing across his lips and he found he couldn't pull away. He dipped his head again, his tongue plundering her softness and warmth, and then she was pressed against him, her fingers entwined in his hair, and Majed found himself lost to sensation.

From somewhere he eventually found the strength to pull back.

Her chest rose and fell as deeply and quickly as his. She touched trembling fingers to her lips and then shot him a shaky smile. 'And I know how much you also like me.'

A laugh burbled in his chest. It would be fun being married to this woman. 'I desire you greatly, *habibi*. I've made no secret of it. But I want you to know that I *like* you too. You've honesty and integrity, and those things are diamonds to me. I think you'll be a wonderful mother— I see the care you already take of our child and it humbles me. A man could ask no more than that. And yet you know how to laugh too, how to make me laugh. I do not think you know how much I value you.'

'Oh!' She pressed a hand to her heart and swallowed. He could see how furiously the pulse in her throat worked. He reached out and brushed his thumb across it. 'Your heart is racing.'

'Isn't yours?'

In answer, he took her hand and pressed it to his chest. 'It races like a wild thing.'

'No man has ever treated me the way you do, Majed. Even when you're angry with me, you still show me kindness and...respect.'

'It's my intention to always do so.' She'd not been shown enough kindness in her life. If she let him, he'd do his best to make that up to her.

'I've a very big question to ask you, Majed. I beg that you'll answer me truthfully.'

His mouth dried but he nodded. They'd promised each other honesty. He wouldn't fail her now.

'Could the people of Keddah Jaleel eventually accept a Western woman as their Sheikha? Would your rule survive that?'

Her earlier unspoken worries made sudden and perfect sense. He nodded, not in assent but in recognition of her concern. 'This is a question I've had to consider carefully. I know it is not *romantic* to admit as much.'

'We're something other than a romance, Majed.'

Her tone was crisp, yet...did she mind? Did she miss romance so very badly? It was true that women loved romance and he'd tried to give her the façade of it—the sunset cruise on the river, this picnic at the oasis…he'd shower her with such treats for the rest of her life. She deserved them. But the two of them weren't a love match. And he couldn't pretend otherwise.

But she *liked* him, and even now that knowledge thrilled him.

'We're something better than a romance,' he told her.

Her gaze dropped from his but when she spoke her voice was steady. 'Yes, we're going to be parents.'

He pulled in a breath. She understood. 'I've thought hard on this issue, Sarah. I'll not do anything that will hurt you or our child, or that'll hurt my country.'

Her gaze met his again. 'It's a big ask.'

'But not an impossible one. I won't lie—there'll be some among the more conservative sections of Keddah Jaleely society who'll try and make an outcry if I marry you—who'll attempt to create outrage in the general population, accuse my father and me of not holding to or valuing the old ways—but we can weather that.'

'How?'

He admired her need to understand. He respected it. If she married him, his people would become her people. And they'd be lucky to have her as their Sheikha. 'My father is popular with our people and his rule is strong. He's only sixty-three. Our line has, thus far, been blessed with good health and long life.'

Realisation dawned in her eyes. 'His rule could last for another twenty years.'

'Or more. Our people will have a chance to get to know you.'

'To grow used to me.'

'While I work side by side with my father, taking on more and more of his duties as he gets older.' In the same way Sarah would take over more and more of his mother's duties. None of them would throw Sarah in at the deep end. Everyone would have ample time to grow used to the idea.

She nodded. 'I see.'

'So what do you say, Sarah? Will you marry me?'

Will you marry me?

The words pounded at her. He needed an answer. Maybe not right at this moment but in a few days' time. And she'd have to give him one.

Her mouth dried. She'd spent several days shadowing Aisha as the other woman had gone about her duties. Sarah's hands clenched and unclenched, that fat file of Rasheed's rising in her mind to plague her. How could she hope to live up to Aisha's grace and confidence? How could she live up to Aisha's inspiring speeches, wise words and innate dignity as she'd visited countless schools, libraries business centres and hospitals?

Majed has told you there'll be time. She didn't need to step into the Sheikha's role immediately...or even in the near future. There'd be time and opportunity to learn all she needed to know.

She'd moved away from Majed to stride around the perimeter of the awning. She turned back to him now. Leaning against one of the tent poles, she curled her fingers around it for support. If she married him, their baby would grow up living with two parents who loved it. *You'll both still love it, even if you don't marry.* But Majed's family were in a privileged position and if she didn't marry Majed she'd be denying her child that position. Could she do that?

And, if she didn't marry him, Majed would be passed over for the throne.

It's not a woman's role constantly to martyr herself in the service of others.

That was her mother's voice, and she agreed with the sentiment, but one could hardly call living in the lap of luxury and getting a chance to study design under a master artisan an act of martyrdom.

What do you want?

She loved Majed.

Would marrying a man who didn't return her love become an exercise in self-destruction?

Only if you let it.

What *did* she want?

She stared at Majed. He hadn't moved. He watched her closely but he didn't say a word. He didn't try to pressure her, just gave her the time she needed. He...waited. In that moment she knew exactly what she wanted. And for perhaps the first time in her life she meant to fight for it.

She lifted her chin. 'Yes, Majed, I will marry you.'

He moved towards her so swiftly she barely had time to draw a breath. He reached out, as if to grip her shoulders or take her hands, but stopped short. She didn't know whether to be disappointed or relieved.

His eyes throbbed into hers. 'Do you mean that?'

Behind the hope she sensed his vulnerability. 'Yes.'

He stared at her, as if he could barely believe it. 'Do you want to consider it for a few more days before we make the announcement?'

'I see no reason for that. You've given me plenty of time to think about it and I'm grateful for that.' She swallowed. 'But now that I've made up my mind I've no intention of changing it.'

'I want to kiss you.' His chest rose and fell. 'But I'm afraid that if I do I won't be able to stop. And we will be seen.' He swallowed, his hands opening and closing convulsively. 'I want the people of Keddah Jaleel to hold you in the highest regard—the way I do. So...'

She blew out a breath, doing what she could to hide her disappointment. 'Well, you better not kiss me, then. But how long do we have to wait for the wedding night?'

She wasn't ashamed of her desire for him, and when his eyes flashed an ache burst to life inside her.

'We'll make it a short engagement.' He took her hand and pressed a kiss to her palm. 'You'll not regret this, *habibi*, I promise you that. Is there any other promise you'd like to extract from me?'

Her palm tingled from the heat of his lips. He didn't release it either and she found it hard to concentrate. 'I...' She swallowed. 'I'd like us to mean our wedding vows.'

'I wish that too.'

A frown suddenly built through her.

'Sarah, why are you strangling my hand?'

Oh! She loosened her grip but he refused to allow her to pull away. 'Are your wedding vows here in Keddah Jaleel the same as the ones we have in Australia? I'll promise to love, honour and cherish you but I refuse to have "obey" in there. This is the twenty-first century and my mother taught me better than that.'

She broke off when he started to laugh. 'We can have whatever you want. I promise.'

She pulled in a breath. 'I just want us to promise to do our best to look after each other.'

He stilled. And then he lifted her hand to his lips again. 'That is not a promise for which you need to wait until our wedding day. I can promise that to you now.'

If she hadn't already fallen in love with him, she would have in that moment. And, when his lips touched her smouldering flesh, she swore that this time they left a mark.

'We must have a betrothal ball!'

Aisha clapped her hands, her delight at Sarah and Majed's announcement a balm to Sarah's nerves, even as the thought of being the focus of a formal event stretched them tight again.

She turned to her prospective father-in-law. Rasheed had paled, the lines bracketing his mouth deepening. His evident lack of pleasure at their news cut at her. She glanced at Majed. How much more deeply must it cut at him?

Rasheed rallied, though. Lifting his chin, he said in formal tones, 'I felicitate you both.'

Her heart gave a sickening thud in her chest. 'Thank you,' she managed to murmur.

Majed stared at his father for a long moment and then bent at the waist to rest his hands on his knees, as if someone had punched him in the stomach. 'Bábá, if it causes you so much pain to see me in Ahmed's place then I will step aside.'

The older man's nostrils flared. 'You'd leave Keddah Jaleel?'

'He'll do no such thing!' Aisha cried.

Majed straightened, meeting his father's stare. 'I'll take up the role I'd have had if Ahmed were still alive. I'll become Samir's advisor instead.'

Nobody said a word.

'Maybe,' Majed started, 'when you see me in my rightful role, you won't be reminded so strongly of the son you lost. Maybe then you'll find peace.'

Sarah shot forward. 'Your rightful place is as your father's heir!' She hadn't known she believed those words until she'd uttered them.

Rasheed lowered himself to an armchair as if his legs would no longer hold him. Sarah dropped to her knees in front of him and gripped his hand. 'I know you love Majed.'

He met her gaze but she didn't understand the heartbreak reflected in his face.

'Your son has taught me a lot this past month about finding my courage.'

He sent her a half-smile. 'You think I lack courage, my dear?'

'I think your heart has been broken and it hasn't mended yet.' Her eyes filled. 'Majed would mend it for you if he could,' she whispered.

Rasheed nodded as if he knew that.

Sarah had no idea how to help mend it either. Her knees hurt. Her back hurt. Her heart hurt. 'What would Ahmed say to you at this moment?'

She rose and took a step back. 'What words of comfort or wisdom would he offer you? What advice would he give?' She gripped her hands together. 'Who would *he* choose to take his place?'

The silence became so deep, Sarah thought she might drown in it. 'I'm sorry,' she finally managed, their white faces spearing into her. 'I had no right to say anything. Please forgive me.'

Majed drew her to his side. 'You're a part of this family now. You have every right to speak up. The decisions we make now will affect you and our child's life and destiny.'

Rasheed's head came up at the word 'destiny'. 'Ahmed would have chosen you to take his place, Majed.'

She could feel the tension crackle from Majed. 'Are you sure about that, sir? Because I'm not.'

Her jaw dropped.

And then Majed turned on his heel and strode from the room.

After three panicked beats of her heart, Sarah swung back to Aisha and Rasheed. 'Will you please excuse me?' she said, before scurrying after Majed.

She caught up with him in the long corridor that led towards the private apartments.

'Not now, Sarah.'

Yes, now, but she didn't say the words out loud. Instead, she faked a cough and pressed a hand to her stomach. 'Will you be a gentleman and see me back to my room?'

He pulled to a halt and glared at her, so she faked another cough for good measure.

'That is not convincing. You're aware of that, no?'

She didn't say anything and eventually he shook his head, but the lines that tightened his mouth eased a fraction. 'You won't be able to make me laugh today, Sarah. So, pray, don't even try.'

She slipped an arm through his and turned him right at the end of the corridor towards her rooms, instead of letting him go in the other direction. 'We're in this together, remember, Majed.'

'That doesn't mean either one of us will not desire solitude from time to time.'

'You can have your solitude in due course, just not right at this moment.'

They'd entered her sitting room but she didn't release him. He glanced at their linked arms and then raised an eyebrow.

'Are you going to run away the moment I let you go?'

His nostrils flared. 'Of course not.'

She let him go and he strode across the room to pour her a glass of water. 'For the tickle in your throat,' he said with a wry twist of his lips.

She sipped it and tried to think of a way to ask him non-confrontationally what he'd meant back there with Rasheed.

'You want to know why I said I'm far from convinced that Ahmed would choose me to take his place.'

She coughed for real this time. She hastily set her glass down and nodded.

'And I'll get no rest until I tell you want I meant, is this right?'

She shrugged. 'Pretty much.'

His chest rose and fell. 'You'll make me say the words out loud?'

Dear God! The expression in his eyes—the pain in them—raked through her. She went to him and pressed her hand to his heart. 'Majed?'

'He betrayed me, Sarah. He knew how I felt about Fatima and yet he still…'

She ached for him.

'I've tried to forgive him. The price he paid far exceeded the crime but…but it doesn't change the fact that he betrayed me—*his own brother*!'

His hand covered hers, his eyes dark and full of confusion. 'He didn't choose me then, and I cannot see that he'd choose me now.'

He peeled her hand away. 'And why should it matter so much still anyway?'

With those words he strode towards the door. His figure blurred as she stared after him. 'Because you still love him.'

He halted and she could almost physically see him count to three before he spun back round. He strode back to her and gripped her shoulders. 'I sent him to his doom! I'm responsible for the misfortune that has befallen my family. How can I possibly take his place with that knowledge weighing on my heart?'

He'd have whirled away again except she captured his face in her hands. 'That's not true. Ahmed made his own choices the day he died. They were poor choices on more than one level. You're entitled to your anger and disappointment, but the fact you still love him—that his opinion still matters to you—tells me he must've been a good man.'

Tears fell down Majed's cheeks unchecked. Her throat thickened and her eyes filled.

'Majed, that makes me think he'd have been truly sorry to have hurt you. It makes me think he'd have sought your forgiveness if he'd lived.'

Anger, pain and despair all warred in his face.

'The two of you were deceived by a clever but wicked woman. Isn't it time you forgave him for that? Isn't it time you forgave yourself?' She pulled in a breath. 'If your positions were reversed, wouldn't Ahmed forgive you?'

CHAPTER TEN

IF THEIR POSITIONS were reversed...?

Majed stared at Sarah. His chest rose and fell, a band tightening about it. He'd have never betrayed Ahmed with a woman. *Never!*

What if Ahmed had met Sarah first?

His hands clenched and unclenched and a shout of pure, possessive outrage boiled up inside him.

'What if Ahmed had brought home a girl who tempted you beyond all reason? What if she let slip that, while she respected your brother, she wasn't really happy...that she didn't love him? What if all her words and actions made you think she had an overwhelming desire for you? Would you have done nothing?'

He stared at Sarah and a chasm opened up before his feet. He couldn't recall the power of his passion for Fatima. Not any more. It had been swallowed by pain—the pain of Ahmed's betrayal, and the utter devastation of Ahmed's death. But the desire he had for Sarah burned like an all-consuming flame through him now. An irrational part of his brain told him he'd kill anyone who touched her.

It's because she carries your child.

Was it?

He took a step away from her, finding it hard to breathe.

'Majed?'

'What you say is true.' He had to force himself to speak, but as he did the resentment that had festered in his chest for the last four years started to drain away. And he let it. He gave thanks for it. He didn't want to hold onto it. He wanted to remember the Ahmed he'd laughed and schemed with…the brother he'd loved with all his heart.

'I can see now how Fatima manipulated us both. Such passion is dangerous.' He took another step away from her. 'It's why I'll never again allow such a passion in my life.'

She took a step towards him but he held up a hand to tell her to keep her distance. Her frown deepened. 'Love doesn't have to be destructive.'

He wasn't taking that risk.

'It's high time I forgave Ahmed. You're right about that. It's been weak and foolish of me to hold onto my sense of injury for so long.'

'You've been neither weak nor foolish!'

Her voice was sharp but he was too busy building a wall about himself—a wall to contain the uncomfortable feelings she roused in him—to heed it.

'What about yourself?'

'What do you mean?'

Her eyes flashed. 'You've forgiven Ahmed. Will you now forgive yourself?'

For introducing a viper into his family's nest? Never!

She folded her arms and glared. She could glare all she liked but she couldn't change the past or undo the mistakes he'd made.

'So...' Her hands slammed to her hips. 'If your father felt responsible for this incident with Fatima, you'd want him wracked with guilt, to lash himself with blame for the rest of his life?'

He'd started to turn away, wanting to escape from her and her too-difficult questions and demands, to escape the far too simple demands of his body, but he swung back now. 'You talk nonsense! My father is in no way responsible.'

She thrust out her chin, her eyes flashing. 'He's the senior member of your family, isn't he? He sees it as his duty to protect you all.'

His mouth dried. *No!*

'It was *his* palace security that failed.'

Majed's heart thumped.

'How old were you, Majed—twenty-five? Your father was a vigorous fifty-nine-year-old who had more experience of politics, rebels and women than either you or your brother. What if he feels he should've protected you better?'

'That is not true! He has always been the best of men and the best of fathers!' The words bellowed from him. 'He has nothing to reproach himself for. Do you hear me? *Nothing!*'

'I know.'

Her soft voice filtered through the tempest roaring through him. He stilled and met those clear blue eyes. 'You do?'

'He has nothing to blame himself for, Majed, and neither do you.'

His heart thumped and pain radiated from his chest. 'I don't wish to speak about this any more today.'

She stared at him for a long moment. That damned lock of hair did that beguiling almost-falling-into-her-eyes thing and he had to bite back a groan. 'Okay,' she finally whispered.

He pulled in another breath. He couldn't leave

her with such fraught words simmering between them. 'I'm glad beyond words that you've agreed to marry me.'

The smallest of smiles touched her lips. 'You're such a big, fat liar. At the moment you're wishing me to the blazes. I expect *glad beyond words* is far too strong for this particular moment. But, I know you were glad. And I know you'll be glad about it again.' She lifted a shoulder and let it drop. 'I can live with that.'

Miraculously, some of the knots inside him loosened. How did she do that? Without giving himself time to think, he seized her shoulders and pressed a kiss to her forehead. 'Thank you.'

Her quick intake of breath speared straight to his groin. And he released her—fast.

She moistened her lips. 'We're going to fight sometimes. You know that, right?'

He took a careful step away from her and considered her words. 'When we feel we're in the right, neither one of us wants to give way.'

She blew out a breath. 'Just as long as you haven't deluded yourself into thinking you're gaining yourself a restful wife.'

He found himself laughing. 'No, *habibi*, I

haven't. A restful wife wouldn't suit me. Besides, it'll be fun to make up after our spats.'

'I'm counting on it.'

She waggled deliberately provocative eyebrows at him and that made him laugh anew. He took another step away from her. 'I must go now.'

She nodded but he felt her eyes follow him as he left the room. He left with a lighter heart than he could've thought possible. And with much to ponder.

Still, it was all he could do not to sweep back into her room and kiss her soundly.

A week later they held the betrothal ball. Majed wore traditional robes that bore the royal insignia in blue and silver. A scimitar in a gilded scabbard set with precious gems hung at his side.

His breath snagged when he caught his first sight of Sarah for the evening.

His. His. His. The word drummed through him in a possessive tattoo.

The traditional tunic that Arras, the master artisan, had made especially for the occasion flowed over Sarah's body in a fall of silken temptation that had him curling his hands into fists. A headdress of precious gems and gold rested against her hair and a ruby the size of a walnut dangled low on her forehead, making her look exotic, unfamiliar...and utterly desirable.

Her eyes went satisfyingly round when she saw him, making his breath jam in his chest. It was her smile, though, that speared him. It was more beautiful than the ruby on her brow.

He lifted her hands to his lips, kissing both of them, letting his lips linger against her soft flesh. She smelled of honey and lavender. 'All the men of my country will envy me when they see you.'

'You...' Her breath hitched as she surveyed him. 'You look amazing, Majed. The single women of Keddah Jaleel will be in mourning that you're no longer eligible.'

She stood in the reception line beside him and welcomed the invited dignitaries and guests who came to congratulate them, charming them all with her warmth and her attempts to speak in Arabic. He hadn't even known she'd been having language lessons! She kept up a *sotto voce* commentary that had him biting back inappropriate laughter, but her grip on his arm betrayed her nervousness.

'You're doing brilliantly,' he assured her. 'Everyone is enchanted.'

'You great big fibber. It's obvious that the jury is still out in some quarters.'

He followed her gaze to the three older gentlemen standing on the other side of the room, all heads of important Keddah Jaleely families. 'We'll win over Omar and Youssef eventually but nothing we do will win Hamza's acceptance.'

She turned that clear blue gaze to him, one eyebrow raised, and he shrugged. 'Back before I was born, Hamza had great hopes that his sister would marry my father. Their family is an old one and the match would have been politically savvy.'

'But your father married Aisha instead. And they've been very happy.'

He squeezed her hand. 'We will be happy too.'

'Of course.'

But her voice wobbled and he gazed at her sharply. 'Come, you should rest for a bit.'

'Oh, but surely that'd be rude and—'

'Nonsense.'

After a quick word with his mother, he bore Sarah off to an empty antechamber and made her sit and drink a glass of the pomegranate juice she'd grown so fond of. 'Not having second thoughts, are you, *habibi*?' He'd do whatever was necessary to reassure her, to quieten her fears and doubts.

'Of course not!'

Her shock calmed the burning in his chest.

'I find being in the spotlight nerve-racking, that's all. Public engagements intimidate me.'

'They'll get easier,' he promised, taking the seat beside her.

She sent him a shaky smile. 'I hope very much you're right about that. Aisha has said the same.'

She'd spoken to his mother about this? He leaned towards her. 'You're truly worried about appearing in public?'

'Doh!' She rolled her eyes but she smiled as she did so. 'You've been born to all of this. I know I'm going to make mistakes and...'

'And?'

'And I don't want them to reflect badly on you. I'm...I'm not used to this level of attention.'

And she didn't like it. The revelation disturbed him. He'd been focussing on all the good things he could give her, the life of luxury she could live if she married him, without considering the sacrifices she'd also have to make.

She shrugged. 'There's a price to be paid for having such a privileged life, and I'll do my best not to let you down.' She drained her glass and started to rise. 'Come, we should get back out there and—'

He pulled her back down beside him. 'You'll have lots of help, Sarah, and you won't have to take on the Sheikha role for many years yet. You'll have the opportunity to grow comfortable in the role.'

She sat back, evidently recognising the worry in his face. 'I know that too. It's why I'm still here. The thought of being Sheikha filled me with fear at first—especially when I realised all that the role entailed.' She glanced down at her hands. 'I don't have a great track record when it comes to holding down a job, so even considering taking on the role seems a cheek.'

'But?'

She glanced up. 'But if I get the chance to follow my design dream...'

'Which you will.'

'Well, that gives me strength.' She frowned. 'And a measure of confidence. If I can be good at that, then maybe I can be good at...at other things. The fact is I'd sacrifice a lot to follow my dream.'

His heart thumped. She was sacrificing a lot.

'You've made that possible for me. It only seems fair that I do what I can to help make your dream come true too. You've the right to follow in your father's footsteps.'

'And you've made that possible for me.'

Taking his hand, she held it against the gentle swell of her stomach. 'This baby has made it possible—for the both of us.'

His hand curved protectively about her. And then he froze, his gaze spearing to hers. She laughed. 'Did you feel that? It was the baby kicking. I believe he or she agrees with me.'

He couldn't speak and she rested her hand over his. 'Majed, instead of running away, I've decided to face my fears and fight for the life I want. It won't always be easy, but I'm aware of that…and you should be too. Please stop worrying that I'm going to change my mind. I'm not having second thoughts. I promise.'

He wondered if he'd ever wanted any woman more than he wanted her in that moment.

She started to laugh then pressed a hand to the centre of his chest and pushed him gently back. 'Oh, no, you don't! You're *not* going to ruin my lipstick. Not tonight.'

So he told her in a rush of Arabic exactly what

he wished to do with her. And what he'd do once they were married.

Her eyes widened and her breath quickened. 'You're... I only understood about a fifth of what you just said but...you're a wicked man, Majed.'

He laughed and took her hand to lead her back out into the grand reception room, pleased with the renewed colour in her cheeks and the sparkle in her eyes.

Majed glanced up from his desk when a knock sounded on the door. He always kept the door to his office partially ajar when not in a private conference. His father's aide stood there, his face grim. Majed motioned him in.

'Your father would like to see you.'

'When?'

'Immediately.'

Majed did his best to hide his surprise. His father rarely requested to see him—their meetings, summits and conferences were all arranged well in advance and entered into Majed's diary by efficient secretaries.

He logged out of his computer and rose, his senses sharpening when the grim expression on the aide's face didn't abate. What on earth...?

Was something wrong? He knew better than to question the man—his loyalty to Rasheed was absolute and his adherence to palace protocols unshakeable.

He entered his father's library, the aide close at his heels. A sense of dread settled in his chest when he saw his father was alone. 'What's the matter?' Fear clenched his gut tight. 'Sarah...?'

'Sarah is well. This has nothing to do with her. Please sit.'

The sense of relief didn't last. The expression on his father's face chilled Majed's heart. 'Abii?' *Father?*

'There's no easy way to convey this news to you, Majed. There has been a sighting.'

Rasheed broke off to drag a hand down his face. Majed leaned towards him. 'Of...?'

'Fatima.'

He couldn't move. He couldn't speak. His heart pounded so hard he thought it might burst.

'We thought she was dead, yes,' Rasheed continued, as if he could read the questions burning in Majed's mind. 'But her body was never discovered.'

They'd thought she'd died, caught in the crossfire between the rebels and the Keddah Jaleel special force that had put down the insurrection. The military had searched the rubble and caves for her body but it had never been found.

'What does she want?' His voice didn't sound as though it belonged to him.

Rasheed's mouth whitened. On his desk his hands clenched to fists. 'Intelligence believes she wants revenge on you.'

On him? He shot to his feet. 'She's the one who led my brother to his death! If anyone wants revenge it should be me.'

Rasheed stared at him stonily, as if frozen. 'When our forces crushed the uprising, her husband and brother both lost their lives.'

Majed fell back into his chair. Against his father's wishes, he'd led those forces. He swallowed. 'She was married?'

His father gave a heavy nod.

Dear God. He and her, they'd... He swallowed. 'This woman is unstable.'

Rasheed met Majed's eyes. 'And very, *very* dangerous.'

The blood pounded in his ears. If she wanted revenge on him, then there was every chance that she'd target Sarah. Fear almost immobilised him, cramping his chest and gut. 'Sarah must leave.'

The words croaked from him. 'We have to get her out of Keddah Jaleel.'

'You must try and think clearly! Sarah will be safest here in the palace. So will you.'

No! He had no intention of hiding in the palace. He meant to find the woman and wring her neck with his bare hands! 'The palace is *not* safe. Fatima infiltrated it once before. I don't doubt that she could do so again.'

'Majed, I—'

He slammed to his feet, his heart burning and his throat constricting. 'She won't go after Sarah if she believes our engagement to be broken.' She'd go after him instead.

Rasheed's gasp sounded loud in the deathly quiet of the room. 'You cannot do that! You'll shame both her and yourself in the eyes of our people.'

He didn't care. He'd suffer any indignity to keep Sarah safe. He'd suffer any fate. The thought of losing her, of Sarah no longer being in the world… He couldn't stand it!

His father surged to his feet. 'This is madness! She will not go. She is committed to you. She is committed to Keddah Jaleel.'

'She won't go if she knows the truth.' He knew

that in the very marrow of his bones. Sarah had her flaws but she was brave—she'd stare danger in the eye and would do what she could to defeat it. He cared for her and their child passionately, and he feared he'd allow his compulsive need for her to cloud his judgement.

He muttered a curse and started to pace. Such need was too dangerous for a man in his position. It put people at risk—people such as Sarah and the baby.

He swung back to glare at the other two men in the room. 'But we will not tell her the truth. Do you understand me?' He met the men's gazes individually. 'Not a single whisper of this is to reach her ears. Do you hear me?'

He trembled with the force of his emotions but could do nothing to contain them. Rasheed finally gave a heavy nod and his advisor followed suit.

Majed let out a breath, some of the tension easing out of him. He'd ensure that Sarah and the baby were safe. 'Leave it to me. I know exactly how to make Sarah leave.'

It wouldn't be pretty, but it would be better than Sarah dying at a crazed woman's hand.

And the sooner he did it, the better. Without

another word he strode from his father's library, his heart growing heavier with every step.

'Sarah!'

Sarah swung round from where she and the women of the female quarters were enjoying a gossipy morning tea. They were bringing her up to date on the political leanings of many of the people she'd met on the night of the betrothal ball. Along with their bad habits, the skeletons in their closets and their secret ambitions.

From what she could tell, no one in Keddah Jaleel had a secret they could call their own.

The smile of welcome that sprang to her lips wavered when she saw the expression on Majed's face. Good Lord! What on earth could be wrong? One of the women beside her murmured what sounded like a prayer.

Sarah stood.

'May I have a word?'

The words snapped from him, short and clipped. Without a word, she followed him from the room, automatically searching her mind for some palace protocol she might've breached in the last few days. She'd been so careful!

She glanced at him and something cold touched

her heart. In Arabic, she said, 'Majed, you look so grim.'

Startled eyes met hers. 'Your Arabic is improving.' He spoke in his native tongue too.

'Shukraan.' Thank you. 'My pronunciation is getting better. I need others to speak slowly to catch what they're saying, but I'm finally starting to believe it'll come and that one day I might be fluent.'

His lips pressed together into a thin line. She didn't understand. Normally he'd be pleased, would congratulate her on her progress. Something weighed heavily on his mind. She'd love to make him laugh—just for a moment—to help lighten his load.

She glanced at him again from the corner of her eye. 'Mind you, we won't mention my written Arabic. Still, I love looking at the script. It's very beautiful, but my tutor keeps telling me it's not aesthetic appreciation he wants from me.' She gave an exaggerated shrug of self-deprecation. 'What on earth could he mean, I wonder?'

Nothing. *Nada. Diddly-squat.*

'If I could find a way to communicate the written word via my sewing machine, I expect it'd make everyone's lives easier.'

He led her to her suite of rooms and then swung to her with a frown. 'I'm sorry?'

He hadn't heard a word she'd been saying! She swallowed. 'It was nothing important.' She sat because she had a feeling she'd need to sit for this conversation.

Majed poured her a glass of iced water and set it on the coffee table…and then paced.

Sarah ignored the water. 'Will you tell me what's on your mind?'

'I'm trying to find the words.' He swung back briefly, his eyes hooded. 'I don't wish to hurt your feelings. I want to give you as little pain as possible.'

'Oh, this sounds promising.' She folded her arms but it did nothing to allay the dread that settled in her stomach.

He sat and went to take her hand but she tugged it free and moved further down the sofa away from him, until she was wedged tight against its corner. 'I don't want you to touch me, not when you look at me like that.' *As if he pitied her.*

'As you wish.'

She could barely believe it when he moved away from her to the sofa opposite. This had the classic hallmarks of a break-up scene. But…that couldn't be possible, surely? They were going to be married in two weeks!

'There's been more political backlash than we expected at my choice of bride. Certain parties are bringing more pressure to bear on my father than we expected.'

'But you both foresaw this would happen.'

'Not to this extent.'

She tried to beat back the panic that wanted to seize hold of her. 'You said Rasheed's rule was strong, that it could withstand a certain amount of disapproval.'

He swung out of his seat to pace again, his face twisting in…fury. Her heart cramped so suddenly it was all she could do to keep breathing. Was he furious with her because…she was questioning him?

'My father is unwell. I don't want him taxed with having to fight this particular fight. It now appears I'll have to take on the role of ruling sheikh sooner than expected.'

She shot to her feet. 'Oh, Majed, I'm so sorry! Is there anything I can do?'

Agonised eyes met hers. 'Go quietly.'

It took a moment for the import of his words to sink in. She sank back to the sofa, her legs shaking too hard to support her. 'Are you...? You're breaking off our engagement?' It took all her courage to ask the question.

He couldn't meet her eyes and maybe that hurt worst of all.

'Yes.'

Acid burned her throat. 'So in the end you choose your kingdom over your child?'

He loved this child. She knew he did.

'My father needs me.' His hands clenched. 'And a man in my position must be prepared to make sacrifices.'

'And what about when this child needs you?' She pressed a hand to her stomach. His eyes followed the movement. 'You promised me friendship and...and respect.' She'd believed him... 'That was all lies?'

He slashed a hand through the air. 'You'll want for nothing. The child will want for nothing. You have my word.'

The child. No longer *our* child.

'Your word means nothing!' She surged to her feet. 'That's neither respect nor friendship. It's simply you doing your paternal duty and nothing more. It's what any man should do.'

She strode around the coffee table until she

stood toe to toe with him. 'You love this child, I know you do, but now you mean to deny it?' If he wanted to be ruler he couldn't admit to having an illegitimate child. It would outrage his people.

Rasheed's words came back to her. *You cannot deny him his child. It will kill him.*

She swallowed and tried to rein in her pain and fear. 'If your father needs to step down then couldn't you…couldn't Samir step into the role? I know it means you wouldn't be ruler, but you'd be a trusted advisor. You'd still have a privileged role leading Keddah Jaleel into the future…and you'd get to keep your child!'

He didn't have to marry her but he could still have a relationship with their child. Surely that was better than the alternative?

'Samir doesn't want to be ruler.' He stared at her with pitiless eyes. 'And why should his life be ruined as well?'

He meant marrying her would ruin his life. Colour leached from the edges of her vision. She retreated to the window and concentrated on pulling in one deep breath after another.

'Your instinct about your unsuitability as Sheikha was, as ever, unerring. I should've heeded it. I'm sorry.'

Flake. Disappointment. Failure. The accusations speared into her. It was obvious she'd been living in Cloud Cuckoo Land. Had she seriously thought she could measure up to the demands that would come with being the wife of such an important man?

'I know I've disappointed you.'

How she hated that voice—so smooth, calm and rational.

'All I can do is tell you I'm sincerely sorry. But, Sarah, this was never a love match. Your pride has been hurt, perhaps, but your heart remains intact.'

She turned at that and lifted her chin. 'Is that what you think, Majed?' She made her voice as pitying as she could. 'Then you'd be wrong. You might have your heart under lock and key, but I'm much freer and more generous with mine.'

He paled. His hands clenched and unclenched.

'The only reason I agreed to marry you—the *only* reason—is because I love you.' She gave a short laugh that nearly choked her. 'You once accused me of cowardice but what an act of courage that was—you'll have to agree—to consent to marry a man who I knew didn't love me back. I never realised I could be so...*optimistic.*'

If possible the lines about his mouth went even whiter, stark in his tanned face.

'I won't let you off the hook that easily. My baby and I will be perfectly fine without you in our lives, but I refuse to allow you to operate under the misapprehension that you haven't hurt us, because you have—deeply.'

He stood there frozen, his nostrils flaring and his hands clenched at his sides. 'There are no words to convey the depths of my sorrow at having caused you such pain.'

At least none that he was prepared to utter out loud. She simply raised an eyebrow—a show of bravado. 'Evidently.'

'I'll make your travel arrangements.'

She turned away to stare down into the serene courtyard below. If he thought she'd thank him for saving her the trouble of making the arrangements, he was very much mistaken. When she finally turned back, he was gone.

She pressed one hand to her heart, the other curved about her stomach. She couldn't think. All she could do was feel. And she didn't want to! Pain scored through her as if a thousand whips flayed her heart. The taste of blood filled her mouth, as her teeth clamped down on her lips to bite back the cries that rose through her. How was it possible to feel so much? How could she bear it?

'Sarah!'

Sarah came back to herself to find Aisha gently shaking her arm. She still stood at the window. The shadows of the courtyard had shifted and lengthened. How long had she been standing here—an hour…maybe more?

'Come.' Aisha led her to a seat and pressed a glass of water into her hand. 'Drink, please. You must think of the baby.'

Oh, yes! She couldn't fall ill. She wouldn't allow her heartbreak to harm her baby's health. She drank the entire glass of water in three gulps. 'I'm sorry, I…'

What could she say—*your son has broken my heart and I'm in shock*? Aisha was his *mother*.

Aisha's eyes narrowed. 'What did Majed say to you? What has he done? I've not been able to get near either Rasheed or Majed all afternoon. They've locked themselves away in meetings.'

She pulled in a breath and told herself to not cry—it would only upset Aisha. 'Majed has broken off our engagement. I'm to return home to

Australia.' Except Australia didn't feel like home any more. Nowhere felt like home.

Aisha rattled off an angry spate of exhortation in her native tongue. 'My son...he is a fool! He loves you and yet he tries to send you away. Why does he do this?'

'He doesn't love me, Aisha. He never did. But I know he loves this baby.'

'Pah, this is nonsense of which you speak. Tell me everything my son said to you.'

She stared into her now empty glass, tapping her index fingers against it. *Fight for the life you want.*

She lifted her gaze to Aisha's. 'You really think Majed loves me?'

'Of course he loves you. It's in his eyes when he looks at you. It's in his every action—though I do not know if he is aware of it himself. He has been frightened of love since that wicked Fatima.'

Sarah's fingers curved into claws. If she were ever to come face to face with the other woman, she'd quite cheerfully scratch her eyes out.

'But you are unsure of his love for you and this is why you let him send you away.'

She'd started to think that, given time, Majed might start to feel something deeper for her. But, that aside, she knew how much he wanted to be a part of his child's life and…

That could *not* have changed so comprehensively.

Aisha shook her head. 'And this is why you do not put up a fight.'

Sarah shifted on the sofa to face Aisha squarely. 'You just said he *tries* to send me away.' She moistened her lips. 'Are you saying that, if I don't want to go, he can't make me?'

Aisha's shoulders went back and her chin came up. 'He is not supreme ruler yet. And I can assure you, my dear Sarah, that the current supreme ruler will *not* dare countermand me on this.'

Her confidence and outrage almost made Sarah laugh.

'Now come, tell me all that Majed said.'

So she told her, finishing with, 'I'm sorry that Rasheed is not well.'

'Pah! It is nonsense. Rasheed has been living too much of the high life, but he is as fit as a fiddle. His gall bladder was removed earlier in the year, but he has recovered beautifully. He is a very vigorous man still, I assure you.'

Sarah's cheeks warmed when she realised exactly what Aisha meant. Aisha patted Sarah's hand with a laugh. 'Just as his son is vigorous… and virile.'

Dear Lord! Where to look?

'But there is something else at work here.'

Like what? If Majed and Rasheed weren't frightened for their country or their rule, what had them so spooked?

'And these men—' Aisha waved her hand through the air '—they think that they can organise the world according to their whim, expect it to run according to their demands and design. Well, they cannot rule us.' She fixed Sarah with her dark eyes. 'Do you have the courage to fight, Sarah?'

Her mouth went dry. Majed didn't want her. And she had no intention of begging him for his love. That would be… It would be too humiliating!

But he did love the life growing inside her. Only a very strong fear would have him sending his child away.

She pressed her fingertips to her temples. Was she just trying to find excuses to make his rejection hurt less? 'Your son doesn't think I can make a suitable Sheikha.'

'What do *you* think?'

Her fears pounded at her. *Failure. Hopeless. Flake.*

But she lifted her head. Majed had deliberately played on her deepest fears. He'd said things deliberately to distance her. Why would he do that?

There was a mystery here and she needed to solve it.

Did she dare…?

Her heart pounded and her mouth went dry. She loved Majed. If he truly wanted to turn his back on her and their child, then she'd leave. But first she had to make sure.

She lifted her chin. 'I think I could make a fine Sheikha.'

'Bravo.'

Sarah reached out and clasped the other woman's hand. 'Aisha, I have a plan—but I'm going to need your help.'

CHAPTER ELEVEN

'WHAT THE HELL do you think you're doing?'

Majed stormed into Sarah's bedroom. It was all he could do not to step forward, throw her over his shoulder and toss her onto a plane himself. Slamming his hands to his hips, he glared at her. She glanced round from the suitcase open on her bed, not looking the least perturbed at his martial tone. That damned lock of hair fell forward, brushing her cheek, making him want to reach out and touch it…touch her.

She gestured to the suitcase as if what she was doing was self-evident. 'Packing.'

His entire body started to shake. 'To go home to Australia?' The words growled out of him in a voice he didn't recognise. They'd been supposed to emerge as a command. Instead they sounded more like a question.

She sent him a look of such pity it made him want to shake and hug her at the same time. 'Don't play the fool, Majed. It doesn't suit you.'

The fool? He started to shake even harder.

'Your mother rang not two minutes ago.'

No doubt to warn her he was on the warpath.

'So I know you're aware of our plan.'

'She's a treacherous—'

He broke off at the glare she sent him. Anger would evidently get him nowhere. He drew himself up to his full imposing height. Thrusting out his jaw, he forced a coldness into his eyes and voice that he was far from feeling. 'I forbid it.'

She stared at him…and then she started to laugh. *To laugh!*

'You've met my mother. Do you honestly think she raised me to put up with nonsense like that? Oh, if only she were here now. She'd have a field day with you.'

She straightened and stuck out one hip. It drew his attention to the shape of her…to her lush curves and the delights her body held. The need to sweep her up in his arms, to kiss her and make love to her, nearly overcame him. But if he did that she'd know—she'd know how he felt about her—and then she'd never leave. *It would put her in danger.*

That was why this kind of passion was so dangerous. It flouted all reason and common sense.

Sarah *had* to leave. There was no other way to keep her safe. He would not allow his passion for her to endanger her further than it already had.

'I'm sorry, Majed, but the moment you broke off our engagement you lost any right to make demands of me—reasonable or otherwise.'

She flipped the lid of her suitcase closed and zipped it up before glancing at her watch. 'You don't have to marry me—that's your right. But you've no right to tell me where I can live or what I can do. You've shown me that I can have a wonderful life in Keddah Jaleel.'

She shrugged. And smiled. *Smiled!*

'I don't have to be married to you to study design and textiles under Arras. I can live here in Keddah Jaleel and give my child a thorough grounding in his or her Keddah Jaleely heritage. We can holiday in Australia. It appears, Majed, that I can have it all.'

But what if Fatima got to her? They couldn't risk it!

He straightened, stiffening every muscle. She'd said she loved him. It would be a dastardly card to play… But her safety was paramount—it was his only priority—and he'd stoop as low as he had to. 'And what about me? You said you cared for me.'

She went to lift her suitcase to the ground but he stepped forward, brushed her aside and did it for her. 'You shouldn't be lifting anything heavy. It's not good for the baby.'

She sent him an odd look—an assessing look—and then nodded, as if satisfied about something. 'Then I'd be grateful if you placed it by the door.' And then she swept past him, out of her bedroom and into the sitting room. 'As for what about you, Majed, I expect you can have it all too. You can marry some Arabian princess that your people will endorse.'

He didn't want to marry an Arabian princess. He wanted to marry Sarah!

Sweep her into your arms. Tell her you love her. You can find another way to keep her safe.

What other way? Marrying him would place her in danger and he wouldn't allow that.

'And you can be supreme ruler of Keddah Jaleel, be king of all you survey and live a blessed life.'

He didn't want a blessed life. He wanted...

If he turned his back on Keddah Jaleel, would Fatima still want her revenge? He squared his shoulders. It wasn't a chance he was prepared to take. Sarah's life was too precious to risk as a stake in such a dangerous game.

'That won't happen once word gets around that my mistress has borne a child out of wedlock.'

'Aisha is confident we can hush that up.'

'You're a fool if you believe that. You want to revenge yourself on me! You want to dash my hopes. I don't know why it should surprise me. After all, it was the way you were raised.'

Her head reared back and he knew he'd scored a point, but it gave him no pleasure.

'I don't see it'll make any difference where I live. You still mean to deny your child. I'll lie for you publicly. So you don't need to fear—your reputation will remain intact.'

'I don't care about my reputation!' He roared the words, fear making his extremities throb.

She came to stand in front of him, her blue gaze unwavering. 'Then what is this about? Would you care to tell me the truth?'

If he told her the truth, she'd stay.

He made his voice ice-cold. 'It's about not being constantly reminded of a mistake that I'd prefer to forget.'

Her quick intake of breath speared into his heart. *I'm sorry,* habibi. *I'm sorry, my love.*

'Cruelty isn't your style, Majed. It doesn't suit you any better than stupidity.' She turned away and wound a scarf—a scrap of sheer chiffon—about her neck. 'Demal is a large city. I doubt our paths need ever cross.' She glanced again at her watch. 'If you'll excuse me, my driver is here.'

What on earth...? She couldn't go to his mother's villa! It was on the other side of the city. He shoved his shoulders back. 'I may not be able to force you to leave Keddah Jaleel, but my father can.'

Her answering laugh infuriated him.

'Good luck with that. He'll have to get through Aisha first, and I don't like his chances. Goodbye, Majed.'

She didn't even offer him her hand.

And then she was gone.

It took two hours before Majed could see his father. His father's aides had to physically restrain him from breaking in on the delicate negotiations Rasheed had been involved in with the delegates from a neighbouring nation. But, when Rasheed was finally back in his office, Majed stormed in and, ignoring everyone else in the room, slammed a fist to the desk. 'You must banish Sarah from Keddah Jaleel! You must have her deported to Australia! She must leave!'

Rasheed stared into Majed's face and then with a few quiet words dismissed everyone else from the room. He motioned to a chair. 'Sit!'

Majed didn't want to sit, but the expression on his father's face had him biting back his anger and planting himself on the chair. 'Has there been news of Fatima?'

'Not yet. I've ordered a dozen men from the special forces unit to be placed around the perimeter of your mother's villa.'

'Have you told her about Fatima?'

The older man hesitated. 'I didn't want to stir up bad memories. She's suffered enough on account of that woman.'

Majed dragged in a breath. 'You could stop this all now if you sent Sarah home.'

Rasheed rested his head in his hands. When he lifted it again, the fine lines fanning from his eyes had deepened. Majed's heart started to pound. His father looked so...tired.

Rasheed lifted his chin but his sigh sounded

about the room. 'Do either of us have the right to make that decision for her?'

'It'll keep her safe!'

'But it will make her unhappy.'

He couldn't deny it...

'How would you feel, Majed, if someone made that decision for you? Would you not be outraged? Would you be able to forgive it?'

Something in his father's voice had a cold hand tightening about his heart. 'What are you talking about?'

'Did you not wonder why I sent you away when Ahmed was killed?'

Acid burned the back of his throat. 'You said it was for my own safety. You said I had to leave to save my mother from more fear and worry. When you didn't ask me to return, when you didn't *speak* to me, I believed it was because you held me responsible for Ahmed's death.'

The older man shook his head heavily. 'I never held you responsible, Majed. It was my fault that palace security was breached.'

'That's not true!'

'Before Ahmed's death, I'd never really understood how dangerous it was to be the son of the ruling sheikh. Oh, I understood it academically, but it had never felt real until that moment. And I knew then that the danger and fear would be present forever. I understood that you were also in danger.'

Majed's heart gave a sickening kick in his chest. 'You...you sent me away and encouraged me to stay away because...'

No. His father would not be cruel enough to let him think he blamed him for Ahmed's murder.

'Because I was afraid of what would happen to you otherwise? Yes. I couldn't face the thought of losing you the same way I had lost Ahmed.'

Majed surged out of his chair. The world no longer felt solid beneath his feet. He lurched from one side of the room to the other. 'But Keddah Jaleel is my home. It's where I belong.'

Rasheed's shoulders drooped, as if a heavy weight pressed down on them.

'I...I thought you blamed me for everything!'

Those shoulders sunk further. 'I know.'

He fell back into his seat, not believing what he was hearing. 'How could you let me go on believing that?'

'I considered it a small price to pay in return for your safety.'

'*Small?* I—' Blood thundered in his ears.

'Your Sarah, although she's not aware of it, made me see how wrong I was. She made me realise I was placing *my* need to keep you safe above *your* happiness. I told myself that you would suffer in the short term but would become reconciled to it all eventually and live a full and long life. And, son…' he met Majed's gaze '…I want that life for you more than anything. But… I placed the demands of my own heart above yours. I'm only starting to see now how wrong that was. I am truly sorry, Majed. I do not know if you will ever be able to forgive me.'

There could be no denying his father's sincerity. He leapt up again, the agitation coursing through him demanding an outlet. 'I… A year ago I'd have stormed out of here and…and I don't know when I'd have spoken to you again.' *If ever.* 'But now that I have a child of my own on the way—' now that he had Sarah '—I'm starting to understand the power of fears I'd not considered before.'

He went to his father and embraced him. 'I forgive you, Bábá. But if you ever do anything like that again…'

Rasheed hugged him back. 'I am glad to have you at my side once again, Majed. You may rest assured that I will never again interfere in your destiny in such a way.'

A weight lifted from Majed—a weight he'd been carrying for four years—making him feel both freer and stronger.

'But...' Rasheed pulled back and met Majed's eyes. 'Can you find the courage to do the same for Sarah?'

He froze. He wanted her safe!

Like your father wanted you safe.

He had no right to take away her autonomy, no right to make decisions on her behalf without her knowledge. His hands clenched. But how would he bear it if he lost her?

He shook his head and spun away. He had to keep her safe, whatever the cost.

But...

He raked both hands through his hair. If his father had held to that course of action, Majed would be back in Australia by now with a wound that would never heal burning in his soul.

He spun back. 'I want to keep her safe!'

'Then work with her to do that,' Rasheed said. 'Not against her. I've had to learn to do that with your mother. And I have to learn to do it with you.'

Majed let his father's words sink in. His heart pounded when he recognised the expression in Rasheed's eyes. Adrenalin flooded every atom. 'You love Mâmâ?'

'Yes.'

'I don't mean simply feel affection for—?'

'I love your mother with every atom of my being!'

It took an effort of will to prevent his jaw from sagging. 'But...your marriage was arranged.'

Rasheed's eyes flashed. 'I fell in love with her the moment I saw her. My father knew that.' His lips lifted in a sudden and sweet smile. 'I made sure he knew it. It's why he selected her from among the other possible choices.'

'You married her because you *loved* her?' Not out of duty, as he'd always thought. The world moved on its axis a fraction. It was love that had made his parents' marriage so strong, not duty, respect or friendship.

'Yes, my son.'

Majed's heart hammered. It suddenly hit him. The real reason he'd wanted to marry Sarah—the reason he'd hidden from himself—was because he loved her, heart and soul. Like his father loved his mother. It was the same reason he'd tried to send her away.

Dear God, had he ruined everything? He spun on his heels. 'I have to go to her. I have to tell her the truth.'

He prayed to God she'd forgive him for what he'd almost done.

He prayed to God that he could keep her safe.

Sarah swam a lazy lap in the sumptuous pool before turning on her back to float. The pool house was attached to Aisha's villa and, the moment she'd seen it, she hadn't been able to resist a dip. She stared up at the tiled ceiling and allowed the cool water to soothe her. The combination of colours—sage-green, cream and dusky pink—helped to ease the burning that gripped her soul.

Majed had been so angry!

She blew out a breath and tried a relaxation breathing exercise, but she couldn't concentrate. She frowned up at those lovely tiles. Something had lain beneath Majed's anger. Had it been fear? She'd thought so...until he'd turned icier than the Arctic. She shuddered now, remembering it. If she let them, her insecurities would get the better of her, but she couldn't heed them. They'd misdirect her.

What do you know for certain?

One: Majed wasn't a cruel man—it wasn't in his nature—yet he'd been deliberately cruel to her.

Two: he might not love her, but his friendship had been sincere. She'd stake everything on that.

Three: he loved this child. She touched a hand to her stomach. *He loves you, little one.*

So…what could he be afraid of if, indeed, it was fear prompting this out-of-character behaviour?

She made a face. It was possible he did fear for his reputation, but she didn't think so. It didn't ring true somehow. In the same way his cruelty hadn't rung true.

So, if he didn't fear for himself, it had to be that he feared for his father's safety…or his mother's.

She frowned. Or hers and their child's. But, if that were the case, why hadn't he told her?

Her heart started to hammer. She straightened and brought her hand down hard, the slap sending water high into the air. *Of all the…!* Because he knew it wouldn't work! He knew it wouldn't make her leave. Her nicely cooled skin heated up again in temper and she slapped her other hand down on the water. Did he think her a child?

A movement in the far corner of the pool house snagged her attention. She turned to find herself staring at a slim and stunningly beautiful woman. All of the hairs on her nape lifted. It suddenly occurred to her exactly the kind of danger Majed might have been trying to protect her from.

Oh, Majed, why didn't you tell me?

Her pulse raced and her heart thundered. She wanted to sink beneath the surface of the water and pretend that nothing bad could happen but...

She had a baby to protect.

She bit back all physical signs of panic that might alert this intruder to her fear. A thread of steel shot through her. She wouldn't let anyone harm her baby. 'Hello,' she said in Arabic. 'May I help you?'

'You are Sarah?'

The woman's English was good, though thickly accented. Sarah considered lying but since the betrothal ball her picture had featured in all of Keddah Jaleel's newspapers. 'Yes.'

'My name is Fatima.'

Then she held up a gun and pointed it directly at Sarah.

Sarah's heart hammered in her throat but she merely resumed floating. *Show no fear. Don't freeze up. Keep thinking.* '*The* Fatima, I presume? I've been curious to meet you.' She cocked her head to one side and considered the other woman. 'You're as beautiful as I thought you must be.'

The woman smirked her satisfaction. 'You have heard of me, then?'

'Oh, yes. You have them all in a flap at the palace at the moment.'

She stiffened and glanced behind her. 'They know I'm in Demal?'

Sarah assumed so. It would explain Majed's ridiculous behaviour. 'They have nothing concrete—at least, not that they've told me. Just rumours.'

Fatima tossed her mane of glorious black hair. 'The security of Aisha's villa is appalling. I could not believe how easy it was to break in.'

Keep her talking.

'Ah, there's a perfectly good explanation for that.'

'Which is?'

Very slowly, Sarah shook her head. 'You first, Fatima. I'll satisfy your curiosity if you satisfy mine. Why are you pointing that gun at me? What threat do you think I pose?'

'Threat?' She gave a scornful laugh. 'None! You are just a pampered Western girl.'

She was neither pampered nor a girl. But she let it pass. She wasn't the one holding a gun. 'So why do you want to shoot me?'

'Revenge,' she purred. 'Majed killed my husband and my brother. He will know the agonies I suffered when I kill his bride.'

Her stomach gave a slow, sickening turn. 'Well, as he broke off our betrothal yesterday, it appears I will no longer be his bride.'

The gun waved wildly in the air. 'You lie!'

'I wish.' She gestured around the pool house—*slowly*. 'It's why the security around here is so lax. You see, Majed was very much hoping I'd be on a plane to Australia by now. He's livid that I'm not. He thinks I'm going to cause him trouble. It's all been rather unpleasant. I couldn't remain at the palace any longer. That's why I'm here.'

Fatima stared at her as if she didn't know whether to believe her or not. She hitched up her chin. 'What kind of trouble could you cause?'

An avid look, almost of madness, had come into Fatima's eyes. Sarah had to repress a shudder. 'Look, do you mind if I get out? It's getting a little chilly in here.'

She might have very little chance of getting the gun away from Fatima on dry ground, but she had no chance at all in the pool.

Fatima motioned with the gun towards the steps at the far end of the pool. 'Any sudden movements…'

'I get the picture.'

Sarah moved up the steps—slowly—until she was no longer in the water and was clearly visible. She turned side-on and stood there dripping, touching a hand to her stomach. 'I think you can see the kind of trouble I could cause.'

Fatima's eyes went wide.

Sarah pointed to her towel—slowly—and then reached for it and started drying her hair—slowly. 'I'm afraid that if you kill me you'll be doing Majed a service rather than an injury. With one bullet you could make this nightmare go away for him.'

Please let her swallow this nonsense.

The gun wavered. 'Why should I believe you?'

'Why risk it when you can verify the truth in the next day or two? I expect the broken engagement will make the headlines. And I'm probably being a little hard on Majed. If you kill me, he will feel guilt and regret, but he won't be heartbroken...and he will be relieved.'

Maria, Sarah's bodyguard who was posing as a maid, entered the pool house. Sarah had thought her own private bodyguard an over-the-top measure, but Aisha had insisted, and she gave thanks for it now. Maria pulled up short when she saw that Sarah wasn't alone. Fatima had pulled the gun down by her side where it was hidden by the material of her tunic. Sarah wanted it to remain there.

Show no fear. 'Ah, Maria, this is...Sinna, an acquaintance of mine. Would you be kind enough to bring us some tea? Or would you prefer coffee?' She turned to Fatima. 'Strong Turkish coffee?'

Fatima gave a short sharp nod.

'Right, Turkish coffee for Sinna, and I'll have some of that lovely chicory coffee.'

Chicory was the code word she and Maria had set up and, to her credit, Maria didn't so much as bat an eyelid. 'Very good, miss. Also, His Highness Majed is on the phone.'

Sarah blew out an exaggerated breath. She had to maintain this charade. 'Can you tell him I'm not available? You can repeat that, as long as he meets my demands, I won't go to the press. Oh, and can you tell him he'll find his mother's coral necklace in the top drawer of the dresser in the guestroom I was using?' She glanced at Fatima. 'The last thing I need is for the palace to accuse me of being a thief.'

'Yes, miss.'

Maria disappeared and Sarah pulled on a blouse. 'She's German. I think they're afraid I'll corrupt a nice Keddah Jaleely girl.'

'She's probably spying on you.'

Sarah shrugged. 'Suits me. If she tells Majed I'm not alone, he'll leap to the conclusion that I'm talking to the press. That suits me nicely.'

'Why didn't you give me away?'

She nodded at the gun. 'Call me sentimental, but I'd prefer not to be shot. I'd prefer that Maria wasn't shot either, even if she is spying on me. She's just a servant girl.'

To her relief, some of Fatima's agitation—the fanatical light in her eyes—receded. 'What are these demands you're making of Majed?'

She gestured across to the patio furniture. 'Shall we sit?' She led the way and hoped that

Fatima would follow, her heart pounding. 'Just money.'

Fatima sat. 'A lot?'

Sarah sat too. 'I think it's a lot. I've asked for a million dollars. I don't care that Majed wants to deny his paternity, but he can jolly well ensure that the child is financially secure.'

'You should've asked for more.'

She still held that damn gun in too secure a grip for Sarah to risk trying to take it from her. 'You think? How much would you have asked for?'

'Two million. In American dollars.'

She feigned dismay. 'I said Australian dollars.'

Fatima snorted her disgust. 'You have no idea what you're doing!'

Sarah slumped back. 'I'm a rank amateur.' *Wasn't that the truth!* 'I've never tried to blackmail anyone before. I—'

She broke off when Maria entered with a clattering tea tray but, before she reached the table, footsteps sounded on the far side of the pool house. Majed strode in, all tall and powerful-looking with those broad shoulders and strong thighs, and Sarah's heart leapt into her mouth. He was such a big target!

'Oh, look, my two favourite women.'

Her gaze snagged with his. Had he heard the nonsense she'd been feeding Fatima? How long had he stood out there listening? She hoped he had the entire villa surrounded with police and bodyguards.

'Plotting my demise, no doubt.'

Don't lose it now! 'Checking up on me, Majed?' She made her words a taunt.

He raised an eyebrow, but she could practically feel his eyes scanning her for signs of hurt or injury. 'Do you blame me, *habibi*? I like to keep my enemies close.'

Fatima rose and pointed her gun at him. 'I'm going to enjoy killing you, Majed.'

He moved towards them slowly with panther-like grace and Sarah's heart pounded. She wanted to shout, *'Turn and run!'*

'Will you kill me quick or will you make it slow, I wonder?'

A scream pressed at the back of her throat. She could see he was playing for time as Maria manoeuvred herself into position behind Fatima, but he was putting himself in such danger!

With a superhuman effort Sarah pulled herself together. She would not let this crazed woman kill the man she loved!

'Do you want to know how Tabor died? Shall I tell you the gory details? Do you want to know whose name he shouted in his death throes?'

Dear God, he was deliberately taunting Fatima to keep her attention on him.

Fatima paled and her face tightened. She cocked the revolver.

No! Nobody was going to kill Majed. She wouldn't allow it.

At that precise moment, Maria flung steaming hot coffee and it hit Fatima in the centre of her back. Fatima screamed, rearing back automatically in reaction, giving Sarah the split-second chance to bring her hand down hard on Fatima's arm in a karate-chop move her self-defence teacher had taught her when she was eleven…and thirteen…and fourteen…and again at seventeen.

The gun slid across the floor and she kicked it away, before catching Fatima in an arm lock that left the furious woman immobilised and screaming in frustration.

'You lied to me!'

She didn't bother responding. She couldn't.

In the next moment, Maria had taken over and a dozen men surged into the pool house. Fatima was handcuffed, hauled to her feet and dragged from the room.

Sarah found herself swept up into strong arms and Majed's lips were pressed to her ear, murmuring words that sounded like a prayer. Arms and lips that made her feel safe, cherished…and loved.

Tears pricked the backs of her eyes. He didn't love her, but he had risked his life for her, and she clung to him now. *He was safe. He was safe.*

'Shh, *habibi*, the danger is now past.'

It was only then that Sarah realised she was crying. 'I—I thought she was going to kill you,' she hiccupped.

He lifted her into his arms, carried her into the house and took her into the sitting room, where he settled on the sofa with her ensconced securely on his lap. He held her close, his hands making soothing circles on her back. She finally pushed herself up a little to stare into his face. 'You were so brave. My heart nearly stopped when you walked in. I wanted to yell at you to run.'

'You were the one who was brave.' He smoothed her hair back from her face, cupping the back of her head and staring at her with such admiration she almost believed he cared for her.

Of course he cares for you. Just don't mistake it for more.

'The way you played for time…played on her prejudices and need for revenge… It was so clever! And you appeared so calm. I was in awe of you.'

'I was shaking inside.'

'I knew you were brave but I've never been more afraid than in that split second when you brought your hand down on Fatima's arm.' His hands gripped her shoulders, his fingers digging into her flesh as his face twisted. 'All I could think was that Fatima would injure you badly—she's expert in martial arts. But you disabled her so quickly and then had her in an arm lock before I was even halfway to you. I—' his hands gentled '—I was never more proud of anyone in my life. Where did you learn to do that?'

Sarah suddenly found that she could laugh. 'My mother, of course. Every year from the age of eleven through to eighteen she bought me a course of self-defence lessons for my birthday. I guess some of it stuck.'

'She is a wise woman. I will tell her so next time I see her.'

Sarah moistened suddenly dry lips. 'Fatima is the reason you tried to send me away?'

His eyes darkened and the lines about his mouth momentarily deepened. 'Yes.'

She tried to shift away but he wouldn't let her. She turned her face towards the door. 'Don't you want to go after them—the guards—to make sure that the woman who killed your brother is—?'

'I don't care about her! I don't care about my revenge! I care about you. I...I care about you, *habibi*.'

She stilled. Her heart thudded. She finally found the courage to turn back and face him. He looked so ragged and vulnerable that she wanted to pull his head down to her shoulder and comfort him the way he'd just comforted her.

'I'm sorry I lied to you, Sarah. It was my father who made me realise how wrong I was.'

She blinked. 'Rasheed? What did he say? I...I thought he wanted me gone too.'

'No, *habibi*, he wanted *me* gone. For the same reasons I tried to make you leave Keddah Jaleel.'

Her heart gave a sudden kick of recognition. 'He'd lost one son. So...he wanted to keep the other one safe. And that's why he sent you away?'

He nodded. 'But you made him see how wrong he was.'

'Me?' she squeaked.

'You forced him to recognise that my home and destiny—my happiness—would always be linked to Keddah Jaleel. He saw that I'd never be happy anywhere else, although I might be safer elsewhere. He realised that he had no right to interfere in my destiny in such a way.'

She leaned back into him. 'Wow.'

'He made me realise I couldn't rob you of your choices and your freedoms either.'

She pulled in a breath. 'You realised that if I knew the truth—that Fatima was on the warpath—that I wouldn't agree to leave.'

'My fear put you in danger. I'll never forgive myself. I should've confided in you and we should've come up with a plan to keep you safe.'

She nodded.

His eyes bored into hers. 'I learned also another valuable lesson.'

Her heart started to race with a different kind of tempo. 'Oh?'

'I can see now how love can make you strong, if you let it.'

Two beats passed before his words sank in. He

continued talking but she didn't hear his words. 'Whoa, wait!' She sat bolt-upright in his lap. 'Did you just say...*love*?'

Midnight eyes stared into hers. His lips curved in a way that made her pulse pound. 'But of course, Sarah. Surely you must know now that I love you?'

She could only stare. And then she could only shake her head.

Very gently he took her face in his hands. 'Little one, you are the light of my life. I love you with all my heart and soul—and very soon I will love you with my body...if you'll let me. If you'll still marry me.'

Of course she was going to marry him...

'I've been fighting it for a long time.' His face darkened. 'I was stupid. I thought love made men weak and easy to manipulate. Not being true to love is what makes a man weak. I allowed my fear of love, and my fear of being betrayed, to rule me. It is those things that made me weak. And it could've ended in disaster. If you had come to harm...'

His regret and self-recriminations tugged at her. She touched his cheek. 'I'm safe, Majed. We're both safe and the threat has been dealt with.'

His hands caressed her from shoulder to wrist, making her shiver. 'Because of your code words.'

'Because we worked as a team.'

He stilled, his gaze burning into hers. 'I want us to always work as a team. I will not make the same mistakes again. I swear that to you. Can you forgive me, *habibi*?'

Her breath jammed in her lungs. 'Say it again.'

He pulled in a breath, his expression intense, his eyes not leaving hers. 'I am sorry. I will never—'

'No, not that.'

He stared into her eyes and then he smiled. 'I love you, Sarah Collins. I love you with all that I am. I will love you forever.'

Warmth radiated through her chest, his words leaving her feeling weightless and grounded at the same time.

'If I promise to honour our vow of love, will you marry me?'

'Yes,' she breathed. 'A million times yes. I love you, Majed.'

She lifted her face to meet his kiss, her arms winding about his neck. She was no longer afraid of having to hide her love from him, no longer overwhelmed at all she felt for this amazing man.

Firm lips captured hers and he kissed her so thoroughly, with such tenderness and intensity, that it made the blood pound in her ears. It left her in little doubt of the depth of his feelings for her.

The baby suddenly kicked, as if to share in her joy, and with a laugh she took his hand and laid it on her abdomen. 'Who'd have thought we would all end up here like this? Who'd have thought an...accident would end so happily?'

'No, *habibi*, not an accident. This baby might not have been planned but it was no accident. It was destiny. It brought you to me, and you brought me home.'

She touched her hand to his cheek, placing her other hand over his on her stomach. 'This baby has helped me find a home—a place where I belong. It has helped me find my courage. While you showed me that I should never give up on my dreams.'

'This baby is a blessing.'

She couldn't argue with that. Reaching up, she pressed a kiss to his cheek. 'Please tell me we can marry soon.'

His eyes gleamed. 'We will be married very soon, *habibi*. I can promise you that.'

And then his lips claimed hers in a kiss that left her breathless, and looking forward to the future with more anticipation than she'd ever dreamed possible.

* * * * *

If you've enjoyed this book,
then you won't want to miss
THE SPANISH TYCOON'S TAKEOVER
by Michelle Douglas.
Available now!

If you're looking forward to another secret
baby romance, then make sure to indulge in
CLAIMING HIS SECRET ROYAL HEIR
by Nina Milne.